Leningrad Nigh

'*Leningrad Nights* is one [...] seems to arrive unmediated from a space located at an oblique angle slightly above the earth's surface. Graham Joyce uses the novella's unique mixture of liberating length and liberating brevity to evoke a phantasmal, haunted version of Leningrad.'

PETER STRAUB

'A dystopian vision of a city under siege. Apocalyptic stuff – writing that takes the metaphors of the Old Testament and gives them the most literal of lives'

DAILY EXPRESS

'Reads like a long-lost urban legend from The Great Patriotic War'   SFSITE.COM

'A superb piece of work'   PAUL BRAZIER, INTERZONE

'Not only extremely well done from an artistic point of view, it's also morally uplifting – a good story in both senses'   CHRIS GILMORE, INTERZONE

'Hard, beautiful and thoroughly engaging, this novella explores the horror of real life, life at its extreme bending the mind to new realities and perceptions'

MICHAEL ROWLEY, WATERSTONES

'The best and brightest from Britain's genre writers. A lavish feast . . . a gourmet treat'   THE TIMES

'Fiction that is blessed by the devil himself'

DAILY EXPRESS

'A good example of what is best about the dark fantasy of century's end'   DREAMWATCH

GRAHAM JOYCE
Leningrad Nights

The right of Graham Joyce to be identified as
the author of this work has been asserted by him
in accordance with the Copyright, Designs and
Patents Act 1988.

This edition published in Great Britain in 2000 by
Millennium
An imprint of Victor Gollancz
Orion House, 5 Upper St Martin's Lane,
London WC2H 9EA

LENINGRAD NIGHTS first published by Victor Gollancz in
2000 as part of FOURSIGHT, edited and with an introduction
by Peter Crowther

To receive information on the Millennium list, e-mail us at:
smy@orionbooks.co.uk

A CIP catalogue record for this book is
available from the British Library

ISBN 1 85798 759 4

Typeset by SetSystems Ltd, Saffron Walden, Essex
Printed in Great Britain by Clays Ltd, St Ives plc

This is the story of a city so old and so beautiful and so terrifying that no one knows its true name. That is, it has many names, but they refuse to harden or fix and set. Every few decades the City fathers have the task of thinking up a new name, one which will last no longer than the others. And each time the name is changed, the city sheds a skin. The skins litter history, and the cities of the old names hover like ghosts, in a time and space of their own.

But what a city it was when Leo was a boy! Where even puberty passed him by, because he was too busy trying to stay alive.

Before it happened, he was a boy happily playing one summer, in a great mythical city of slender golden spires and dazzling cupolas and secret waterways. He fished, all the time; he could talk the fish on to his line. Then the sky darkened and there was the nine hundred days siege. Then he was a man. The nine hundred days taught him everything this world had to teach him, and by then he was still only fourteen years old.

His father was killed very early in the war. It crushed

his mother so deeply that it crippled her spirit and she
surrendered the will to live. She was one of the first
victims of the siege, contracting dysentery and dying of
infection. Later he would thank the guts of the martyrs
that all Russians were not so weak, or the nine hundred
days would have been the ninety days and the Nazis
would have been swilling vodka in the Winter Palace
before the end of the first Autumn.

'Weak,' croaked Uncle Yevgeny, as they buried her.
They were still burying people properly at that stage. He
made a minimalist gesture with his hand. 'She was
weak.'

When Yevgeny croaked like that, it was not out of
sentiment. Uncle Yevgeny was a gnarled, bitter old Russian with a face carved from a bulb of knotted pine. He
drank tea soaked in tincture of opium and lived alone up
by the Museum of Atheism. His throat had been cor-
rupted by smoking thick twist low-grade Turkish tobacco;
now he only ever croaked or growled, or more typically
abandoned speech altogether. Mother had disapproved
of him, but now he was all Leo had left.

'What must I do, Uncle? What must I do?'

'Do?' Yevgeny said, turning from the fresh grave.
'What must you do? You must stay alive.'

That was the only advice or help he ever got from his
uncle. Everyone else was preoccupied with surviving the
siege. He stopped going to school and no one seemed to
notice.

He was already accustomed to shortages. There had
always been a shortage of this or that and rationing had

been introduced long before the Nazis were hammering on the gates. He'd been raised with an ability to improvise, to eke out whatever was there, and he could barter like a Cossack. But nothing could have prepared him for what was to come.

Vast guns, hunkered like grey wolves on the dark horizon, pounded them from the German lines; usually with clockwork regularity, and then sometimes at any hour, just to keep the Russians on their toes. Sometimes it seemed they were making a joke out of the bombardment. Every day they would shell precisely at six o'clock for one hour, over several days. It was like waiting for the rain to give over before you could go about your business. Then one day for laughs they would start an hour early, or pause before slipping in an extra burst and everyone would be sent scurrying like rats. The guns taught Leo a lesson in the absolute laws of uncertainty.

The people would crawl out of their houses to assess the damage: this family's house demolished, or a cinema gone forever. And while everyone was full of sympathy and patriotic anger, they were secretly relieved that it was not their own miserable hovel that had sucked in the whistling shells. There would be smoke everywhere. Ribbons of dirty blue or yellow smoke suspended, unmoving, in loops and coils three feet above the street, or hanging in the blasted doorways and broken windows of the wrecked houses.

Leo did what he'd been told to do. He concentrated on staying alive. He prayed, and not to God, but to the blind justice of The Whistling Shell, that he and his house

3

might be spared but that it might take the Godenuvs because they were dirty and known thieves, or the Kuprin family because their eldest boy now fighting on the lines had bulled Leo at school. And if he was right – and sometimes he was – he thanked the blind justice of The Whistling Shell with a selfish heart, and promised to offer up another prayer the next day, if only he might be spared.

He hoarded; anything he could get his hands on: food, firewood, matches, salt, anything which he saw was becoming scarcer. In the streets people were selling their watches, their jewellery, whatever might bring in a crust, but Leo hoarded. It got so bad that the people ate their horses. Then when they had eaten the horses, they ate what the horses ate. They ate rough oats. They even boiled up grass with the oats to make it to further. Leo learned about the colour of shit after he had eaten grass.

In desperation he turned to Uncle Yevgeny. Even though there were things about the district which scared him, he made his way to Yevgeny's apartment to beg for help.

There was no electricity to light his way as he clambered over rubble and squeezed through the blocked stairway to Yevgeny's freezing apartment. A rat scuffled on the steps, and on the third floor the handrail on the stairs swung out over the stairwell, and Leo went with it. Somebody had taken the banisters for firewood, and Leo swung out over the dark stairwell and back again as the handrail opened and closed over the death drop like a pair of shears.

Already in a state of shock, he stumbled into Yevgeny's apartment, finding the door open. Yevgeny was seated in his usual chair, gazing out of the frozen window at the ice-bound river Neva and the Museum of Atheism.

'Uncle?'

Uncle didn't stir. His eyes were open, but the frost on the window had jumped across the room to ice his blue eyes. His hands rested in his lap, bearing a shred of cardboard. Another piece of cardboard was in his mouth, but dry. Leo wondered how many hours his uncle had been sitting there.

'What do you do, Uncle?' Leo tried to imitate Yevgeny's guttural inflections. He stood behind the seated corpse and nudged Yevgeny's elbow so that his dead uncle's bluish hand flicked in a tiny gesture. 'You survive.'

Leo left Yevgeny gazing at the golden dome of the Museum of Atheism.

There was nothing edible to salvage from the apartment. Instead Leo went to the cupboard where he knew his uncle kept the samovar. What a vessel it was! It had been in the family for generations, and it had always been a matter of chagrin to Leo's mother that the samovar had fallen to Yevgeny. On the few occasions when the family had visited, Yevgeny used to take down the samovar for all to admire, and, Leo observed, to annoy his mother.

'It's too fine to make tea in!' his mother would protest.

'I agree,' Yevgeny would growl, proceeding to do so anyway.

5
.

But it was true: it was too unique an object to spoil with use. The silverwork was a delight and the porcelain was decorated with pictures of serpents harried across the earth by the fiery sword of a winged saint. 'Everything that makes our family special is written on that samovar,' Leo's mother would complain bitterly after every visit. 'All my memories of childhood. Your babushka, Leo, and even my own grandfather. All my memories kept alive under the engraved silver lid. I wanted it for the family ashes, and Yevgeny cooks up his stinking brews in it!'

He would no longer. Leo took down the samovar from the shelf and wondered what he might get in return for such a beautiful object.

'Bye, Uncle,' he said, bearing the samovar out of the apartment.

'Uggh,' he croaked on his uncle's behalf, a passable personation of the old boy's minimal salutations.

Leo had no misgivings about parting with the object. His guts were clawing with hunger and besides, everyone in his neighbourhood had made sacrifices of their most personal possessions, and he felt a pleasant righteousness in joining the people in communal suffering. It was fitting. He could hold up his head.

After bearing the samovar home, he waited indoors until the pounding of the guns was over, so that he could go out when most of the people would be out of doors. Then he carried the samovar proudly into the street, plainly affording everyone equal opportunity to view this splendid artefact before they put in their bid.

He found a knot of old men and women on a street corner. They were surveying a building that had sucked in a shell. It had been a tailor's shop, and now it was a pile of rubble. Grey smoke writhed like a serpent over a broken tailor's dummy, and thence along the litter of plaster and broken lath and smashed masonry.

He marched confidently up to the whispering crowd. 'What will you give me for this rare and beautiful samovar?' he asked, thrusting the object under their noses.

They looked, first at the samovar, and then at him. Then they looked at each other. Then they laughed in his face. 'What's the use of a samovar without any tea?' cackled one of the old women.

Stung, Leo advertised the ceramic drawer at the back of the samovar, where he had seen Yevgeny keep his opium-soaked tea.

One of the old women peered into the drawer. 'What's that? Mouse droppings? The lad's trying to pass mouse droppings off as tea!'

'Here!' said another. 'Come into my house. I'll give you some mouse doings.'

One of the men inspected Yevgeny's tiny twists of tea. 'You sure it's not your own doings?' he said. They all laughed again.

'It is tea!' Leo roared. He felt his cheeks flame and his eyes water. Hunger gnawed his bowels like a rat. He had marched out to make a sacrifice of his family's most treasured possession, thereby to join the suffering of the people, and the people had laughed. He was paralysed

7

with humiliation. He couldn't even make a move to run away or hide his face.

One of the old men approached him and steered him away from his tormentors. 'No one wants a samovar,' he said gently. 'Take it home.' Leo only looked at him angrily. 'Wait here,' the man said, before going into one of the nearby houses, returning with a rough biscuit.

'One small biscuit for this?' Leo stammered.

'Look,' the man said, 'I'm only trying to save your face in front of these old women. A samovar is worth less than nothing in this city now, and maybe never will be again. Give it to me and take the biscuit; then at least you can walk home with your head up. What do you say?'

But Leo thought he was being cheated. He couldn't see that the man was acting out of kindness, and that things were going to get even worse. 'Peasants!' he shouted. 'You're all too stupid to see the value of this samovar!'

The mood of the small crowd turned. He now realised he'd made a mistake in drawing attention to himself. 'You make sure you eat that biscuit,' said another woman, 'because tomorrow it'll be your turn to go to the line. Make yourself useful and kill a few Germans.'

'Give me a gun and I'll go now,' he said, his thirteen-year-old voice cracking.

'You'll have your gun soon enough. This tailor,' she said, indicating the still-smoking ruins of the shop, 'was already measuring up your uniform. Now we'll have to find you another tailor.'

He didn't know at the time, but they didn't have any

guns; and that if they had, then he would already have
been sent up on the line.

'Meanwhile,' said another of the old women, for
they'd rounded on him now, 'why don't you take a leaf
out of o' those Young Pioneers' books, and stop whining
about self self self all the time.' She was referring to a
band of boys and girls who went around the city trying
to help people in their suffering. 'Don't think we haven't
noticed you scurrying in the shadows like a canal rat,
trying to pass off samovars to folk for what little they've
got. Don't think it hasn't been noticed. Get out and help
folk if you can't fight and you've got nothing to do with
your time.'

He was stung with tears. He ran from them, ran back
to his house with the wretched samovar, and flung
himself on the bed, sobbing, the breath gone out of him.
His heart was lacerated with shame. He hated the old
crones. He wanted to die. Hunger tore at his belly and
the reproach of the old women echoed cruelly in his
ears.

He regretted not accepting the biscuit, for he'd nothing
left. Leo opened the ceramic drawer and surveyed the
tea ruefully. Soaked in Yevgeny's tincture, it had indeed
been compressed into tiny pellets. He used one of the
pellets to brew himself a cup in the beautiful samovar,
and when he drank the cup of tea he'd made, his hunger
pains subsided almost immediately.

Tea-coloured; and gold; and immeasurably older than
ever he'd suspected the city to be. That was how it

9

appeared to him when he went outside. The entire city
gone the colour of, well, if not tea, then perhaps stale
chocolate, but with a soft pulsating under-radiance. And
a double-image, as if there were now a second Leningrad,
this one inaccurately superimposed over the first one he
had known; but he knew without doubt that this new
version was the real Leningrad.

He took with him a flask containing more of the tea.
He floated through the streets like a wraith, marvelling
at the architecture still standing and the demolished
buildings equally, seeing a rhythm in the spaces between,
an exceptional order to the dispensations of The Whistling Shell. And the staircases revealed by half-blasted
walls were everywhere, proliferating and multiplying
until he could see through walls to all the staircases in
the entire city, vertiginous stairways, flights of steps,
dizzying ladders, criss-crossing fire-escapes, comprising a
kind of music and proportion. Astonishing to see so many
hundreds and hundreds of staircases running up and
down. He walked until his neck ached from gazing up at
them.

He found a small girl, maybe four years old, grubbing
in a pile of bricks. She wore a dirty blue smock and was
half-starved. Her eyes were disproportionately large for
her face and she looked at him with suspicion as he
approached. When she asked him for something to eat
he offered her a sip from his flask, which she took before
running off into the shadows like an alley cat.

The act of dispensing that drop of narcotic tea made
him feel whole again. Unable to shake the image of the

girl from his thoughts, he returned home, his heart in shreds for love of her dirty blue smock and her hunger. He saw it very clearly: a new Leningrad had been triggered, in which he could be a new person. He resolved from that moment on to spend his time looking for people to help, to seek out suffering and to do what he could wherever he could. He'd been stung into action by the bottomless eyes of a tiny girl. No longer would his own hunger, safety or comfort be the motivating principle of his life.

And there was suffering. Everywhere. His eyes had suddenly been opened. The people were dying like flies. Winter had locked in the very breath of the city and the lung-cracking cold was unbearable. If they weren't dying of starvation, the people were freezing to death. In one street he encountered the body of a woman solidly frozen in a standing position: she had leaned against a wall, exhausted, snow-covered, no food to keep her going, and had fallen asleep on her feet. She just never woke up.

He went about the city trying to do good, helping here and there, finding a stick of fuel for this old person, scratching a bite of food for this family. He became well-known: they called him the red-faced angel. In the places he visited, he was very glad to see a rat. He became an expert rat-catcher, skinning them and stewing them, perhaps with a potato. With melted snow he made pans of stew this way and took it to hungry people.

'What is it?' they would invariably ask.

'Best steak,' he would say without a wink, and they thought it wonderful.

11

He ventured out every day, fuelled only by the occasional sip from his tea-flask. The houses were dead. The city was becoming choke-full of ghosts, smoke hanging in the air and the reek of death and piss and shit everywhere in the sreets. It was not unusual for him to stumble across corpses lying in the snow. The apartments stood like grey tombs in a necropolis, all intersecting with tracings of weird staircases. Sometimes he had to break down doors to find if anyone inside was alive.

The fact is that half the population was lost. A million people. By the end of the nine hundred day siege the body-count would be nearer a million and a half. He moved through the dying, seeing the spirits of the recently dead ascending from the bloated or frozen corpses without egress. Ectoplasmic forms stuck to ceilings and door lintels like deflating grey helium-filled balloons. He talked to them, whispering encouragement, suggesting routes through the flickering and ethereal morass of staircases.

He had one good coat but he gave it away and adopted a soiled blanket, clasped at the neck with a talismanic twist of shrapnel. He thought if he wore a piece of The Whistling Shell, the dermis of the Kruppsteel God, then he might be passed over. He was himself surviving on next to nothing. He consumed very little of the meagre food he turned up; he was running on another fuel, the light and heat and energy of the inner flame, the fire of the soul. It seemed enough, and it got him from house to house, day to day. He was inspired by love for the suffering people, by self-sacrifice and untiring hard work.

It goaded him on through the ghost city, through the slums and ghettos, grey smoke weaving and coiling about them like worms. All this suffering, the Germans, the smoky serpents; they fused together in his mind to represent a single common enemy launching all these attacks from a platform high above the city, an enemy which could be defeated if only it were possible to keep the inner lamp burning.

And he had an ally in his work. On the radio, they continued to broadcast the sound of a metronome ticking, an act of defiance, to show that the city still had central control somewhere, a heart beating bravely. Ghost broadcasts crackled over the airwaves to be followed by the dull relentless ticking of the metronome. Loudspeakers set up in the glacial streets carried the eerie rhythm. Sometimes he kicked open the doors of houses to find only corpses, or old people weak beyond speech; but the radio would be turned on and the metronome ticking. It was like the numinous presence of a minor god; Tempo, trailing audial banners the length of the march of time, reminding him that even the grey wolves at the gate would turn to fur and bone and dust. If he could out-survive them.

And his ally came in the shape of the stirring words, broadcast over the airwaves, of the boy-poet. Whatever Leo was doing he would stop and listen to his inspiration. The people talked of the boy-poet, said he was only eleven years old, but his poems rang with courage and patriotism, with defiance and exhortation. His words fell like a momentary sweetness amidst all the

13

rot and despair and the decay. They were food and fuel to the soul. It didn't matter how deep into the hell they were falling, the poet's words were a parachute for the heart.

Leo loved the boy-poet, whoever he was. When he was weary and heartbroken from going about his business, the boy's words reminded Leo of his mission. He envied his spirit and faculty. Such wisdom in such youth! Leo carried his words with him like a flag wherever he went, memorising them and discussing them with the people he helped. The boy-poet betokened Leo's faith, his certainty that one day they would win through. Leo, who had never before written a word of poetry, found himself scribbling pale imitations of the poems he heard on the radio.

Then suddenly one day the boy-poet stopped broadcasting. Leo listened for an explanation, some report of the boy's circumstances amid the diminishing bulletins. There came no word. After a while he went to the radio station clutching a sheaf of his own poems to show the boy-poet and to find out why he had ceased broadcasting. He was received there by a gruff, consumptive, unshaven man who wore one half of a pair of spectacles over his right eye. 'The boy-poet? Maybe he's dead.' There was the rot of vodka on the man's breath. 'What have you got there? Let's have a look.'

The radio-station manager squinted through his single lens, giving Leo's poems the once-over. 'Hmmm. Maybe he's still alive after all. Listen tonight.'

That evening the same boy's fearless young voice

crackled over the airwaves, but this time Leo recognised the words as his own. Leo brewed himself the last of Uncle Yevgeny's tea, and wondered how that could be. Then the answer came to him. The boy was not any one individual, but the living heart and soul of the city itself, choosing with arbitrary conviction to speak through this person or that. And the man from the radio station had told him that he, Leo, had brought the boy back to life. Leo threw himself into the enterprise of poetry with augmented passion.

Though he dreaded the idea of returning, something propelled him back to his Uncle Yevgeny's apartment. He needed to make a search of the place, even though he would have to climb over the man's putrefying corpse. He had no idea of what conditions he might find it in.

Though there were patrols, there was little looting going on in Leningrad. What was the point, when everyone was trying to get rid of their material possessions in return for a bit of bread? The door to Yevgeny's apartment stood ajar, exactly as he'd left it. The wind whistled through a window where the glass had been blown out by a shell, casting flurries of snow inside the room.

Leo was astonished to find Yevgeny's cold body in fine condition. Certainly the skin was the blue colour of heated steel, but there was little evidence of decomposition. Someone had explained to him that this could be caused by the creation of a micro-climate. Leo felt the cold air circulating around the room and sniffed the body for evidence of decay.

'I'm still here,' Leo croaked with uncanny accuracy. He had to suppress a smile at his own talent for mimicry.

It was true. The old man's glassy eyes were still fixed ahead on the ice-bound Neva and the Museum of Atheism. 'So I see, Yevgeny, so I see.'

'*Uncle* Yevgeny. Show a bit of respect. You're still a pup.'

'I'm a different person now, Uncle. I'm doing some good.'

'You think you can do good? No one can do good. You'll find out. What are you doing? Keep off my things.'

'I'm looking for your tea, Uncle. You must have stashed it away somewhere.'

'You stole my samovar, you little whelp. I'll come after you.'

'You'd better not. I've been around a bit since we last spoke. I've seen a few things.'

'You've seen nothing. When I was in the trenches fighting for the Tsar we had to cook and eat the enemy before we were through.'

'And I'll take this old army coat of yours if you don't mind. You won't be needing it.'

'Put it back, you dog. I saluted the Tsar while I was wearing that coat, and I saluted Lenin. None of them were any good. Keep your grubby little paws out of those pockets.'

'Ah, tea! Magnificent! I had a feeling it was in here. And medals, Uncle! I didn't know you were decorated. Mother never told me you were decorated!'

'Your mother was weak little slut with a runt offspring.'

Leo turned and fisted Yevgeny hard in the face. The impact forced the frozen head to the side. Yevgeny looked downcast. 'Don't ever speak of my mother again in that way, Yevgeny.' He re-aligned the head so that Yevgeny could continue to gaze upon the Museum of Atheism. 'I'm sorry to have be part of your moral re-education, Uncle, and I regret not having time to complete the job. But I have important work. I may not be back this way for some time.'

Leo pulled on the greatcoat, took the tea and decorated himself with the medals.

'And your slack-mouthed juvenile poetry is piss in the wind,' Yevgeny shouted as Leo left the apartment.

Leo went about the city doing good wherever he could, seeking out opportunities to help people. He never disclosed to anyone the fact that the radio station had chosen to broadcast his words, fearing it an arrogance. But he encouraged discussion of the boy-poet's passionate appeals. Yes, they agreed, his words are a source of unflagging inspiration to us all, and no, he had lost nothing in nobility of thought or in the power of his invective.

Leo was almost delirious with a mixture of humility and pride on hearing the suffering people speaking about his poems as they came over the radio. Humility and pride. And perhaps that was when the split first occurred.

Sheltering one day from the early evening chorus of
The Whistling Shell, he sipped at his tea-flask and composed poems of metronomic metre with a tiny stub of
pencil as the agents of pride found their way in. Hiding
behind the crump of gunfire and detonations, they
winged in on the mortars and infiltrated with the stealth
of grey smoke. Leo wrote a line and scratched it out;
wrote and scratched. But he was already lost. The whispering of these unseen agents had already found ear. If
he could bring the boy-poet back from the dead, they
reasoned, could he not also restore life to others? There
is no death, he wrote in his notebook. Humility scratched
it out. Pride wrote it in again, this time in a firmer hand.

When the evening bombardment had given way to the
canticles of the howling wind, Leo ventured out again.
From that moment on he went from house to house,
seeking out the worst cases, the near-corpses, the death-
in-life situations, the most hopeless conditions in which
he could work.

The cold and ice raged. That winter of 1941–42 had
fangs of crystal and steel. The people he passed in the
streets wore full-face masks to protect their skin from
being stripped by the wind: red masks, blue, green, black.
Lustreless eyes looking back at him from the peepholes
cut in the masks. The trolleybuses stood dead on their
tracks, hung with ice, creatures of extinction. Leo had to
give up poetry when the ink froze in his inkwell and his
last centimetre of pencil vanished in his hands in the
middle of a sprung rhythm. He was still finding bodies,

stiff as sticks frozen in the street having given up the ghost on their way home after collecting water from holes hacked out of the Neva ice.

His search for the worst cases took him to the Haymarket district. Around the Haymarket the scum and cut-throats of Leningrad plied their business. He was afraid, that was certain. He was, after all, still a boy and at that time rumours of cannibalism were rife. Everyone would claim that they knew someone who had a friend who had had one of their children abducted by the cannibals. Everything at that time was believable. Was there cannibalism in Leningrad during the nine hundred days siege? One does not ask questions to which one already knows the answer. And the stories insisted that the cannibals prized child-meat above all other. It was dangerous to wander around at night. But guided by the inner flame, he was drawn to the worst areas of the city.

Perhaps the ghouls left him alone because they thought he was mad. A filthy thirteen-year-old boy, shuffling along in Yevgeny's over-sized greatcoat, deco-rated with pre-revolutionary honours. And he argued with himself as he went about his way. Impassioned debates ostensibly to keep himelf awake or to prevent himself from drifting into the gold and sewer-brown narcotic mist of the alternative Leningrad. Sometimes it happened that his tiring spirit would lose an argument with himself, and the humble spirit within him would shelter under a broken stairwell, to sleep, to dream, while the proud and angry spirit would split away, racing

GRAHAM JOYCE
. . . .

contemptuously from one phantom staircase to another
in the massive over-arching gallery of the transparent
city.

But while the humble spirit dozed, the split would not
endure for long and the haughty spirit would return,
apolegetic, having found from somewhere a meaty,
savoury stew, hot and steaming, with which to revive his
brother. And the humble spirit, not knowing if this was
real or an apparition of the fuel of Good Work, would
accept it anyway. 'What is it? Is it rat?'

'Best steak,' the haughty spirit would reply without a
wink. 'We can do nothing if you die on me.'

So perhaps the ghouls left this mad boy alone as he
made his way through the corrupting shadows of the
Haymarket. Maybe some race-memory of the deranged
antics of the shaman scared them off. For whatever
reason the scum and the spivs, the pimps and the detritus
of the worst of all wars in the coldest of all cities eyed
him suspiciously and with polluted eyes, but allowed him
to pass unmolested.

Then, in one apartment, lying on a bed of filthy rags,
he found a young woman, skinny and dystrophic, but
pregnant and very close to her time. She couldn't even
move from her bed for sickness and cold and hunger.
Another twenty-four hours, Leo figured (and how he'd
become expert in making these assessments as he moved
among the sick and the dying), and she would have
joined the one and a half million.

What was miraculous was that the baby was still alive
inside her. He placed his hand on the woman's distended

belly and felt it move. This he took as a special sign: this one was for him. The woman's eyes failed to register him as he knelt by the bedside. Her spirit had already died and only her feeble body anchored it to this world. Exactly what he was looking for. He, Leo Shapoval, thirteen-and-a-half years old, would take it upon himself to bring both her and her baby back from the dead.

He took her hand. She was grey with cold. She couldn't have been much older than eighteen or so herself. He tore down some old curtains and piled them on the bed. Then he went out to pillage neighbouring houses for anything that would burn. While levering a door from its frame he was spotted by a looter patrol, and fired upon. They gave chase but he escaped. After an hour he returned with several strips of broken lath, made a fire and boiled up some water.

His first act was to trickle some drops of opium tea into her mouth, before taking a sip himself. Then he set about changing the bedding. It was soiled and filthy, so he burned all that and put down fresh bedding for her. Her clothes stuck to her body. He undressed her completely, took a rag soaked in the boiling water and washed her like a baby from head to foot, hoping that some feeling might be restored to her limbs, or that some lustre would return to her eye. There was not a flicker of hope.

He rushed out into the street again. He desperately needed to make her a thin broth, something that would revive her. He was confident that of all of the people he had helped, someone would now come to his aid. But he found no one who would part with so much as a grain of flour. They had nothing; or they pretended to have nothing, and they turned their shamed faces away from him. Now they could no longer look him in the eye, those who had once laughed at him. He was frantic. He went about for three hours. Then he found a man baking bread. Bread! He watched the man bake his 'bread' from sawdust and glue. Sawdust and glue and a fingerful of flour. The man promised Leo a slice – and one slice only – when it was baked. After a fight someone gave him a potato.

He made a soup of the potato. Then he went back to collect his promised slice of sawdust loaf and crumbled that into the soup. He dipped his finger and let the soup trickle into the girl's mouth. She coughed, but eventually she swallowed it, and then she took some more. What was left he set aside for later, but he knew it was hopelessly inadequate. He needed meat. Just a little. Just enough to give her and her baby some strength.

Ground meat was available at the Haymarket, at fantastic prices. Three or four hundred rubles for a few patties. It was always patties, for who knows what goes into a patty? The people who sold the patties were always big men with heavy boots. And they were invariably fat, with soft, pink cheeks, while everyone else around them was a floating wraith. Something about the soft, pink and yet leathery texture of their skin gave rise to speculation. But it made no difference. The price was utterly beyond his reach. He despaired.

'It's no good,' he said aloud. 'She's too far gone.'

The proud boy sniffed from across the room and tossed

another stick of wood on the fire. 'Not this one. This one is mine.'

'I'm sick of it,' said the humble boy. 'I'm too tired. I can't do this any more.'

'And I'm sick of your constant whining. Why don't you stay here. I'm going out.'

'Don't!' The humble boy's head was nodding. 'I know what you do.'

'Stay here. Look at her. Write a poem. Get some sleep.' And with that the proud boy ran up a flight of tea-and-gold coloured stairs, and was gone.

'What do you know about pregnant women, Uncle? What can you tell me about childbirth?'

The late winter sunlight lanced off the golden dome of the Museum of Atheism and reflected from the icy crystals of Uncle Yevgeny's eyes. The effect was one of the remarkable iridescence. 'I don't care about pregnant women,' Yevgeny wept. 'Look what they did to my leg.'

Leo glanced down and winced. Someone had amputated Yevgeny's left leg at the knee. Neither was the amputation a surgical operation. The job had been performed frantically, perhaps with an axe.

'You won't be needing it, Uncle. You're not going anywhere.'

'It's not right.'

'I've got more important things to worry about. What can you tell me of childbirth?'

'What do I know? Have your boot laces ready.'

'My boot laces? What for?'

'You'll figure it out.'

'You're an old shit, Uncle. You know that? A frozen turd.' Leo stood behind the corpse of his uncle and sniffed. Still no signs of decomposition. He aligned himself with Yevgeny's view of the Museum of Atheism. 'What do you see there? Tell me what you see every day.'

'I see Isaac.'

'Who?'

'You're an ignorant little communist-reared brat. That is the cathedral of St Isaac. I see the saint rising out of the dome, an inch at a time. One day it will be a cathedral again. Oh, my leg! My leg!'

When he returned to the house his small fire was winking out in the grate. He fed it the last of his fuel and tossed whatever he'd found into the pot. He was shivering with exhaustion, and knew that he had to find a way to keep both of them warm. Stripping off his own damp clothes he climbed into bed beside the skinny woman. She was the first woman he'd ever seen naked, and she was not a pretty sight. Undernourished, feeble, sickly, skin hanging on bone and an ugly swollen belly like a pig's bladder. It was not an erotic experience for young Leo.

Finally he fell asleep, cradling her to him, trying to think warmth into her. He refused to let her die. He knew that if she died, then it would also be over for him. Once in the night he woke up and thought she had finally let her spirit go, but no, she breathed again. The wind outside moaned and complained at a soul dropped in transit, a spirit fumbled, but the woman had chosen to come back to him. All through the night he rocked her, holding life into her, keeping her just centimetres from the dark precipice.

The next day the same. He washed her with hot water and trickled some of the meat broth – yes it was meat – into her mouth, and he fancied that he could see some colour coming back into her sore limbs. The second night he embraced her to him. This time he woke in the freezing night to find her arm locked tightly around him. Her clinch was unbreakable, but he knew that the impossible had been enacted: he had loved her back to life.

That next day something sparked in her eye, a brief flare, tiny, but in the cosmos of her iris a comet travelling across the loneliness of space. She took in his presence and looked about the room. She placed her hand on her belly to feel if the baby was still there, and seemed dismayed to find that it was. He gave her a little more broth, perhaps too much, or maybe it was too strong for her, because she vomited it up again.

'Come on,' he said, 'that's my best steak.' But she was too weak to smile, let alone answer. Her rejection of the food notwithstanding, after a week of tender nursing she was coming back to life.

Later he gave her more of the broth and this time she kept it down. Leo looked out of the window with satisfaction. Down in the smoky, tea-coloured, snow-

shrouded street stood a boy in an army greatcoat
bedecked with campaign medals. The boy waved back at
him.

He had other things to worry about. The baby was
about to arrive.

The girl shuddered and wept and uttered the name of
some saint he'd never heard of. Then she spoke her first
words to him. 'Go and get someone who knows what to
do.'

'I'm your only hope,' he told her.

She cursed him. Her second words to him were a
volley of filth. He'd never heard anyone speak quite that
way, alternating between appeals to saints and demons.
He didn't mind in the least: wasn't he her saviour? She
groaned as a contraction came and he tried to comfort
her with lines from one of his poems.

'Believe in the future, because the future for us is the
present.'

She stopped groaning when she heard that, squeezing
her eyelids together as if trying to focus on him. Then
she threw back her head and cackled manically. Her
laughter unnerved him. There came a scratching at the
window, and there, outside in the dark, floated the
doppelgänger-boy in his army greatcoat, shaking his head
in dismay.

He ignored the apparition suspended at the window.
'Tell me what to do,' he said, 'because there's no one
else.' In truth he could have gone to find some old
woman to come and boil water and administer to the

whole messy business, but he was committed. She was his, and the baby was his.

Yet he knew nothing of life other than what the siege had taught him. He knew how babies got to be where this one was, and he wouldn't have minded the opportunity to practise with someone to make another. But the business of how they emerged, or how to get them out . . . He was utterly ignorant.

But he had with him the blessed elixir, the divine poppy juice. Already schooled in its best effects, he let her sip tea from his flask in judicious doses, and though she still moaned with pain she was able to ride her contractions like a small boat on the barrel of a wave. A gelatine-like fluid formed over her eyes and her manner softened. 'What's in that tea?'

'Never mind that.'

She reached out a hand and tousled his hair. 'Whatever it is, you little runt, you're a fucking saint.'

He took a pull on the tea himself, and the first ten hours was easy enough. He swabbed her and held her hand. He recited lines which he told her soared from the pen of the boy-poet. She tolerated this for a while until she exploded from within her opium cocoon to protest, 'Give it a rest, will you?'

'I thought the words of the boy-poet would be a comfort to you.'

'That radio-fuck? I hate the whining little milksop. I always have hated him – him and his piss-quick doggerel. I can't believe you remembered his words just to bring

27

them to my maternal bed! What fucking abominable luck! In the name of Judas give it a rest!'

'Don't you like poetry?'

'Fuck! Jesus and Judas! Mary's milk! Not another line, please!'

'Fine. I won't say any more.'

She was the first person he'd met ever to claim open hostility to his free verse. It was a salutary lesson in literary criticism. But he had little time for authorial sulking, because her contractions increased and her waters broke.

'More tea, little brother, more tea!'

Like a tempted saint, he had so far managed to keep his eyes averted from her vagina. Now as she drew up her knees and opened it to him, he was terrified. It was as if he'd secretly hoped that the baby might be spewed up from her mouth, but as he squinted in horror at her distended labia he felt he was peering at the Gates of Life: smooth, living and pulsating pillars of pink, mottled porphyry, veined with marble and grown around with a rampant ivy. It was the notion of what lay within or behind these gates that intimidated him, for he knew that they gave passage into a shadowy damp cavern glistening with the mercurial rivulet, the herald trickle, and that the cavern itself gave way to a roaring cosmos in which solar blizzards buffeted and shrieked with cold hard energy and blinding starlight. He backed away.

But the baby was coming, and he was gripped with an irrational terror that when it arrived it would be demonic, but resembling him exactly, fully formed at his present age and that there would be an exchange of souls where he would have to take the baby's place sheltering in that solar blizzard of energy, waiting for the next opportunity to be born.

He saw a purple bulge appear, and there and then he made a prayer and a poem and a dedication and a promise on that baby's head and on the safety of his own soul that he would spend the rest of his life devoted to doing good. How was he to know it wasn't the baby's head he was looking at, but the distended tissues of vagina and anus. He'd sworn his most profound and dizzying oath on the spare flesh of an arse and a cunt.

But the baby did come, and when it did it shot out of her and right into his hands, milky with vernix. It was so slippery he almost dropped it. The energy blizzard, the shrieking of the raw cosmos behind the Gates of Life, got louder in his ears. He hadn't been prepared for the baby's colour, which matched the tone of Uncle Yevgeny's cadaver; or for the slightly conical head, which, even as he stared at it, seemed to be resetting in orthodox fashion; or for the small black lakes of its eyes which fixed on him and blinked with unconvincing cinematic animation. Moreover there was a membrane on the baby's face, a caul. It didn't seem right and, instincts taking over, he stripped the caul away with his fingers.

The woman lay groaning on the bed. He knew that the umbilical cord couldn't stay there holding the two together so he plunged his knife in some water he had boiling and made to chop it.

'Not yet!' she panted.

He waited. The afterbirth eventually slithered out like a sack of blood and tripe. The shrieking and roaring from the aperture of life went on unabated, louder even.

'Tie the cord in two places,' she said above the noise he was hearing. 'Where is your string?'

String was the last thing he'd thought of. String was for preparing parcels for the post office, not for equipping babies for life. Then he remembered something Uncle Yevgeny said, and he unlaced his boots.

'Tight,' she said, 'tie it really tight.'

He tied one of his laces near the baby's abdomen and the other further down the umbilical cord. She motioned that he should cut. He cut, and the shrieking stopped. But for the breathing of the new mother, and the soft feathering of snow at the window, there was no sound. He held the baby in his arms and it blinked at him with an expression of perplexed relief.

'What is it?' the woman wanted to know.

He looked at its blue-grey skin, its bruised head, and said, 'What do you mean?'

'Is there anything between its legs, you fool?'

He peered hard, and for a long time. 'Only the usual.'

She laughed hard, and sat up. 'Give me the baby. Here. It's a boy.' She fell back laughing, holding the baby to her breast. 'Only the usual.'

Leo was shocked by the sound of laughter. He couldn't remember when last he'd heard it. He too laughed, and he ran to the window, opening it to the soft billows of snow. 'May I, Leo Shapoval,' he shouted joyfully to the dark street, 'announce Only The Usual.' Then he closed the window again.

But the laughter stopped for both of them, because there was more to do. 'I must get clean,' she said.

The maternal bed was a hideous mess. Leo stared at the sack of afterbirth, almost as big as the baby itself. Perhaps it was because she was starving, or maybe she knew it was good for her: whatever, she stuck her hand into the afterbirth and stuffed some of it into her mouth, gagging on it at first, but then swallowing. It made Leo want to vomit, but she didn't even seem to think about it as she wolfed down another handful of the stuff.

After she'd told him to dispose of the rest of the placenta, he cleaned them both. First the baby, which he wrapped in one of his mother's traditional babushka scarves he'd brought from the house. Then he cleaned up the mother. She'd had a bowel movement during the delivery and the blankets were soiled with blood and shit.

'Pretty messy,' he said.

'You try it sometime.'

'I'm not criticising. I was just thinking: it's a pity everyone can't be a mature witness to their own birth. After all the shit and blood, everything from this moment on is progress.'

She looked at him hard, and stroked his cheek. 'You're all right, kid. I don't know who the hell you are, but you're my guardian angel. Thank you, Heavenly Father, for sending him! What did you say your name was?'

'I'm Leo. Are you of a religious bent?'

'I'm Natasha. I think we should call this baby after you.'

He looked at the babushka-wrapped miracle of warmth and breath. He was beautiful. 'Can we call him Isaac?'

'Sure we can. Isaac. What day is it? Do you know? Does anyone still know?'

He had to thumb through his notebook to work it out. 'It is December 21st.'

'Longest night. Now the days will get longer and the nights will get shorter. Leo, I feel our luck is changing.'

She made him keep the caul.

Leo could see that Natasha was a very rough kind of woman, hard-bitten and coarse-mouthed, even at her young age. But all that counted for nothing. Natasha was his sleeping princess. She was the property of fable.

'Who are you, Leo?' she asked him repeatedly.

'Can't you see it doesn't matter who I am? I've brought both you and the child back from the brink. Together we have cheated death!'

'Listen, Leo. I'm going to have to disappoint you now. I'm afraid you've saved a whore and a whore's brat. Do you know what a whore is? It means you've saved less than nothing.'

'Nonsense!' he cried. 'It doesn't matter what you were before the war. The past is all aflame. The march of future will be our present – '

'Fuck the saints! Will you please stop speaking to me in poetry! I can't stand it!'

'What I mean is, things can be different now.'

'You're young. Very young.' The baby started to cry. 'Look, Isaac can't get enough milk. I'm not strong enough to be a mother to him.'

Leo looked across the room. There his doppelgänger waited, nodding his head. 'I'm going out to get something to eat. You'll be all right.'

'Promise you'll come back, Leo? Promise?'

'I promise.'

Leo went directly from there to the Haymarket vendors. Patties were still on sale at mythical prices. Natasha had told him to take the caul with him.

'What on earth for?'

'If you put it about that you have a baby's caul, someone might give you something for it. It's considered good luck, especially to the sailors. They believe it's a charm to prevent them from drowning.'

But no one was much interested in a caul. The fat, soft-skinned spivs looked at him with contempt, wrinkling their noses. One bald-headed trader of expensive furs and shrunken beetroots leered at him. He had the eyes of a dead fish. 'But a good-looking boy like you can always earn himself a patty in five minutes.'

'How?'

The spiv stuck out a blue slug of a tongue, waggling it lasciviously.

'Fuck your mother on a dark grave,' shouted Leo's doppelgänger from over his shoulder. The fat spiv only shrugged and stamped his feet against the cold.

Leo made his way to Uncle Yevgeny's. Someone had

made a fire in the downstairs doorway. He had to step over the wet ashes. 'Ho, Uncle,' he cried, when he got upstairs. 'You don't look too good.'

'My arm is gone,' Yevgeny protested. 'And how am I suppose to balance if I lose my other leg?'

'Hey, that reminds me. Your advice about boot laces. Came in very handy. Got any more tips about child-raising?'

'Drown them at birth. They'll never do you any good. One day they'll break your heart.'

Leo put his nose close to Yevgeny's neck. 'Oh! I do believe you are finally on the turn, Uncle. You'll be no good to anyone. Still, it was good while it lasted. I wonder what changed.'

'They burned the door, downstairs. It affected the through-draft.'

'Why are you talking to a stiff?' asked the doppelgänger.

'He's a better conversationalist now than he ever used to be,' Leo protested.

'Hey! Less of the abuse!' growled Yevgeny.

'It makes me sick to hear you chattering away to a decomposing corpse.'

'I agree he's on the turn,' Leo said, 'but just occasionally he has a useful contribution to make.'

'Get what you came for and let's go.'

'Ow! My last leg!' Yevgeny shouted.

'Damn it, I cut myself,' Leo said.

'Get out of here,' said the doppelgänger. 'I'm going to torch the place.'

34
. .

'Is that necessary?'

'Of course it is. With that front door burned off you don't know who's going to walk in and find this old bugger. There will be questions asked.'

'Before you go,' Yevgeny groaned, 'look in the drawer. Something for Natasha. Not that it will do you any good, for you're beyond all redemption.'

Leo opened the top drawer of the writing table. There were two books. One was a pre-revolutionary army-issue Bible. The other was the Comrade's Guide to Civic Duty. Leo took both. The doppelgänger was tearing up floor-boards and stacking them under Yevgeny's chair. Leo got out. He was two hundred metres away before he turned and saw flames flickering in Yevgeny's apartment.

'Leo, you work wonders. You really are a saint. Where do you get all this? I've never eaten so well in months. Where do you get it from?'

'I made lots of contacts. People know me.'

Leo had moved Natasha and her baby out of the unsavoury Haymarket hovel and into the family home. In turn she cleaned the place thoroughly, made it more like the dwelling house it used to be. It was superior to anywhere she'd ever experienced, and she said so. He showed her his mother's best linen, and the silverware, and the samovar. 'You're too trusting,' she told him. 'Most whores would steal everything you've got.'

'So? Steal it. I've learned that I don't need any of it. Anyway, you're not like most whores.'

'What do you know, you little runt? Don't look at me

that way! When I call you names it's a joke. Try to see it
as a sign of affection. What exactly is in this broth we're
eating?'

'Best steak.'

'So you keep telling me. Far be it from me to complain,
Leo, you work miracles, but I think this time it's on the
turn.'

'Shall I pour it away?'

'Are you crazy? We might not see the like for another
six months. I only make the observation. And now my
milk has come in properly Isaac is thriving. It's just that I
can't help being curious about where you go.'

'All right. There are rumours around that the ice road
is proving more successful every week. The occasional
truck gets through. I think I've noticed an improvement,
but it's more than I dare to speak about.'

'The ice-road!'

The ice-road was almost mythical. A perilous fog-
bound sheet of glass, forming, breaking, re-forming to
allow the sporadic relief convoy to squeeze between the
blockade, a finger of relief prised between the windpipe
and the frigid Nazi death grip. Some doubted its existence; most believed, and in their minds the ice-road was
supernatural in its manifestations, a plumed serpent dip-
ping from between the stars of the galaxy, or an irides-
cent leviathan sinking beneath the ice and rising again.
The need to believe in the supernatural was strong, a
survival reflex deep in the group mind. Useless rationality
itself was rotting, ready to fall away like the spare inch
of umbilical cord days after a delivery.

'The ice-road!' Natasha whispered to suckling Isaac.

Leo shivered. If he was going to give her hope like this he was going to have to make the ice-road more successful.

Natasha turned to him. 'Do you know what day it is tomorrow?'

He shrugged. 'Wednesday maybe. Or Saturday.'

'I'm going to show you something. We'll go out.'

'You're not well enough to go out!'

'Yes I am. My strength is returning.'

The following evening Natasha wrapped Isaac against the cold. She insisted they go out during a bombardment. 'No one must see us. Let's go now the shelling is at its heaviest.' The guns pounded from the lines and the shells whistled softly as they pummelled the town. Natasha led Leo to a place near the Summer Palace.

She led him to a library he recognised, though without her revealing a downward flight of steps, he would never have known of the cellar beneath. She pushed open a door to reveal an untidy circle of people, each of whom held a lighted candle against the dank and dark of the cellar. They looked up instantly, and with frightened eyes.

'Natasha,' one of them breathed. 'It is Natasha! We thought you were dead!'

The group instantly relaxed, embracing Natasha in turn. There were four elderly men and seven or eight women of different ages. 'So few of us now!' Natasha said.

One of the elderly men spoke up. 'We don't know

who is dead, or in whom the spirit has died,' he said, hugging her fondly, 'but it warms my heart to see you tonight.'

Leo hung back, holding little Isaac, until Natasha beckoned him forward to be introduced. They shook his hand or kissed him and fussed the baby as if it were the last infant on earth. 'He's one of us,' Natasha said of Leo proudly. 'He doesn't know it yet, but he's one of us.'

'What's that?' Leo wanted to know.

The oldest man, a patriarch called Nikoli with a forked, iron-grey beard said, 'I'm sorry but we don't have a lot of time. We would like to be through before the bombardment ends.' A lighted candle was thrust into Leo's hand and he found himself drawn into the circle. 'On this special night,' Nikoli intoned, 'we thank you for bringing your daughter Natasha back to us, for her son Isaac, and for our new brother Leo. Each new or refound soul is a grain of light in this dark place, added to the general store. We ask for strength in the coming trials.'

The group murmured an answer to this appeal and began to sing. For fear of being discovered they sang in very soft, muted tones, and words that Leo had never heard before, but which Natasha knew by heart. Then Leo noticed something strange happening. During the singing, one of the group put down her candle, leaving it to burn on the floor, and she left without a word. A few moments later another member of the group did the same, then another. Soon there was only Nikoli and Natasha singing, with Leo gazing dumbly on. When they'd finished, Nikoli said, 'You go now and I'll follow in a few minutes.' He began to extinguish the flickering candles with his thumb and forefinger.

'Tomorrow?' Natasha said.

'But of course tomorrow!' Nikoli answered with a grin, but in the orange candlelight Leo could see that his leathery face was lined beyond all care. Then Natasha was tugging his sleeve. They left silently and were half-way home before the bombardment ended.

'Fuck the saints, I'm freezing!' said Natasha when they got home, 'but wasn't it worth it?'

'What are they?' Leo asked. 'Some kind of devil-worshippers?'

Natasha's face fell. 'Are you joking?'

'Of course I'm joking. They're Christians, aren't they? As you are. I knew. Even though you said you were a whore.' A light died in her eye when he said that, so rather quickly he asked, 'How did you know they were going to be there?'

She smiled again. 'It's Christmas Eve, of course! You didn't know that. Why should you? It's a special day for us.'

'But I did know, in a way. Here, I brought something for you.'

Leo had wrapped Yevgeny's army-issue Bible in a silk scarf of his mother's. Natasha accepted the gift, but before unwrapping it she stared hard at Leo and then flung her arms around him, smothering him in kisses.

'Stop it! Stop it! You haven't opened it yet!'

'But it's Christmas, Leo; it's what people used to do at Christmas. They gave each other gifts, and I have nothing for you!'

'You already gave me Isaac! Open it!'

She unwrapped the silk and her jaw dropped. She stroked the cheap binding, turned the Bible over and over, as if it were hot to hold. 'You know the trouble you could get into for having this?'

'I can't see why. I had a quick look at it, and it didn't seem to make much sense.'

'Where did you get it?'

Leo didn't have time to answer because there came a hammering on the door. Leo was paralysed. It had been so long since anyone had knocked upon his door that he didn't know what to do. Then Natasha lifted up her skirts and, almost by sleight of hand, spirited the small Bible away.

Leo moved to answer the door, opening it just a crack. Outside was a military man in a greatcoat. He wore a seaman's cap. 'Are you Leo Shapoval?'

'Yes.'

'I heard you've got a caul.'

He led the sailor inside and introduced him to Natasha. Leo spotted a movement in Natasha's eyes when she saw the man, but thought little of it. The sailor had overheard that a young boy had been trying to sell a caul in the Haymarket. He'd traced Leo here.

'We never see sailors these days,' Leo said.

'I got sick leave. Got a ride in a truck that came through the ice-road,' said the sailor.

'The ice-road,' Natasha murmured to Isaac. 'So it is true.' She seemed to bury her head in her baby's clothes.

'It's getting easier to break through,' said the sailor. 'Look, I don't have much money, but I can offer a few things.' He produced from his duffle-bag two apples, a tin of corned beef, a packet of dried figs and a bar of chocolate. What do you say?'

'Wow!' said Leo. 'I'd say we accept. Natasha?'

Natasha turned her face to the sailor for the first time. 'Of course we accept,' she said boldly.

Leo got the caul and gave it to the sailor, who held it in his hand as if it were a crystal in which he could see a dry future. Then he prepared to go, but before doing so he turned to Natasha. 'Have we met before?'

'No,' said Natasha, too firmly. 'We have never met before.'

The sailor coloured. 'My mistake. I'll be on my way. Thank you for the caul. May you all survive.'

Leo saw the sailor to the door. When he returned Natasha was strangely quiet. Her eyes carried the inward stare. 'God bless all the sailors,' she said. 'God bless the ships at sea. God bless all the men who have sailed in me.' Then she wept.

Leo, understanding none of this, said, 'Hey, sister! No need to cry! We've got all these good things the sailor brought. We've got each other. We've got Isaac!'

But that only caused great shuddering sobs to wrack her body. 'Are we in hell, Leo? Have we done bad things? I have been so wicked in my life.'

'We're all of us selfish, Natasha. All of us.'

Natasha sobs became hideously mixed up with laughter. 'You! You're a saint, Leo! A fucking angel! That's what upsets me so. I don't deserve you. If God has chosen to send me an angel then I must be so deep in hell that He is afraid I will never get out.'

'But I'm not an angel. And I don't believe in God.'

'But you're more of a Christian than any of them! If you have a coat, you give it away. You feed others before you feed yourself. You wander the scorched earth looking to do good. You go out of your way to help vile rubbish like myself.'

'Don't say that! I won't hear it!' Leo was on his feet. Now it was his eyes that were wet.

'I'm sorry. Come here, let me hold you.' Leo submitted his head to be cradled by her free arm. Isaac seemed to stare at him wide-eyed from his position at the other breast. 'Shall I tell you why I believe? The communists hate a whore. They said I was the worst kind, the original capitalist parasite. We won't mention that Lenin was a frequent punter at the Leningrad brothels; and I could tell you things I've heard about Uncle Joe Stalin that would make your skin crawl. And I spent two years in a re-education camp, with my head shaved, where my communist mentors called for my services in the night. One of my educators lectured us about the fetish-value of gold in a capitalist society during the day. At night he would make me wear a pair of golden high-heeled sandals. He always asked me how much I used to charge men in my old life. Then the pig would bend me over the table. Yes, it was quite a re-education. My arse would be so sore and he had me repeat over and over, "M-C-M" and "C+V+S" and all those things. Do you know what it means?'

'Not really.' Leo had become subdued. She stroked his hair.

'Something about surplus value and commodities. I never understood why they wanted us to know all that. But anyway it was at the camp that I met a woman, there to be re-educated because she was a Christian. She told me that Jesus loved whores and had a special place in his heart for a slut in the Bible called Mary Magdalene.

'She told me many things. She didn't need a Bible, it was all engraved word for word in her heart. We used to say "JC+MM=L". Love. We had private communion where she showed me how to eat the body and the blood of Jesus.'

Leo's ears pricked up. 'You did what?'

'We ate the body of Jesus. It's called Holy Communion. Tomorrow I will take you back to that place and we will all take the communion together. What's the matter, Leo, you look strange.'

Leo got up and filled the samovar with water. He had a hundred questions, but he couldn't ask any of them. 'Nothing. My stomach hurts. I'm going to make some special tea.'

'I thought you never would.'

The next day, being Christmas Day, there was no shelling. The haphazard deity of The Whistling Shell gave way to the discriminating God of The Middle-Eastern

Shepherd Cult, but it gave the citizens of Leningrad no peace, because all day long they assumed it was a German trick, a ruse, a feint. The Hun, they were certain, would be sure to punish the communists for their atheism by slipping in a few mortars at the exact moment of the putative saviour's birth. Though even this was problematic since the despised and deposed Eastern Orthodoxy decreed that the saviour had sprung from his mother's virgin loins at precisely twenty minutes before six in the morning, whereas the Catholic or Calvinist Germans were rather more vague about the exact moment in which an unending ray of light entered this world.

They didn't seem to think it might have been twenty to six, Leo considered, since he was awake at that hour, and all was quiet. He'd been unable to sleep since Natasha had told him that they were to spend the day gorging on the cadaver of the saviour, if he had understood things right. But Natasha had also told him that the Germans, being not of Eastern Orthodox persuasion in these matters, had a looser idea about the exact moment of the nativity. That, it seemed, was more in line with his notion of the random dispensations of The Whistling Shell. Lying awake in bed that Christmas morning, his mind was already turning on a synthesis of the two creeds, one in which The Whistling Shell was sucked into the bosom of the suffering servant in an act of supreme sacrifice.

As he understood things from Natasha, there was the Father, the Son and the Holy Ghost. The first of these two were pretty damned clear, but the last figure in the trinity was a much more shadowy identity. Could this have been another name for the Kruppsteel God of The Whistling Shell? The point about the indiscriminate proclivities of The Whistling Shell was that in its dispensations it also triggered the random acts of kindness which motivated Leo in his wanderings throughout the city. Perhaps this could be rendered as a Marxist-style formula: F+S+WS. He was unsure. He would have to ask Natasha, who knew more about these things.

He became aware that Natasha, lying next to him, was awake and looking at him. Isaac, snug and warm between the two of them, slept on. 'What are you thinking?' Natasha asked. 'You are always thinking!'

Leo was about to answer, but she placed a finger on his lips. 'Never mind. I want to say something. In the night I woke and I cried because I had no gift to give you on Christmas Day. You, who have given me life, and my son's life, and your constant care and love. Why, you even troubled in all of this to find me a precious Bible. And I have nothing to return.'

'It doesn't matter.'

'Shhh! Let me speak. It was then, in the night, that I remembered I do have something very special to give you after all.'

She lifted Isaac, still sleeping, from between their bodies and laid him at the foot of the bed. Then she turned to him, her grey eyes like woodsmoke.

'What?' Leo said. 'Why are you looking at me like that?'

She kissed him. 'You're so sweet, Leo. You don't even know what it's for.' She reached down under the blankets and gently closed her fingers around his cock. He flinched immediately, but she held on to him. His breath came short as his cock started to fatten in her hand. 'See, Leo? You only need a little help.'

He was speechless as she teased him to full erection. 'I'm too sore and damaged from giving birth to Isaac,' she whispered, 'but there is some other thing I can do for you.'

Natasha planted a row of kisses down his chest. There was a cloying perfume that made him think, inexplicably, of dark orchids in the glasshouses of the State Horticultural Institute. He yelped when she slipped his cock into her mouth, thinking she must surely be planning to bite it off; perhaps as part of her perverse communions and body-eating rituals. But she stopped what she was doing, reassured him, stroked his cheek tenderly before resuming. It was while he shuddered, wide-eyed with pleasure and terror, that across the room he saw the doppelgänger, a shivering, ice-clung, hoar-crusted boy gazing back at him, astonished, incredulous.

Ignoring the doppelgänger he closed his eyes, abandoning himself to her. She was like an orange flame burning on a landscape of snow as she worked away; her mouth like a hot wind around an ice-fountain. And then he heard it. Or perhaps he only thought he heard it. One solitary whistling shell, falling softly from the sky, slow and drawn-out as it tumbled from the vortex of heaven, trilling and piping in the cold air until, in a sudden, tumultuous acceleration, it exploded in the street out-side. Leo opened his eyes momentarily, to see the blast suck the doppelgänger clean out of the window.

The congregation had one or two less for the Christmas Day service than had been present for the previous evening's ceremony. The sense of disappointment was palpable. The patriarchal Nikoli referred to it in his informal talk. 'What can we do? They're starving, they're sick. Just to find the energy to move around consumes all their reserves. We'll pray for them.'

And after a prayer Nikoli said, 'Perhaps we are, all of us, being tested. Perhaps all of our suffering is a test, just as our Saviour was tested with suffering. Perhaps God wants to know how many of us will fall when so tested. And how tempting it is, under the burden of our suffer-ing, to take the easy way, to want to steal, to cheat, to lie if it advantages us in some small way. Perhaps God needs to know what we are made of, deep down; to see who can still walk in the narrow beam of light our Saviour introduced into this dark world.

'But only think of this, brothers and sisters! How God will remember; and how we will remember for all our lives, the ones who, having so little, give freely of what little they have. Because he who can come through this test without falling, he will banquet for ever at the table of the Lord.'

Then Nikoli produced a silver chalice in which there was a spot of sour cloudberry wine, and a silver salver bearing few crumbs of bread. 'The body and the blood,'

GRAHAM JOYCE

said Nikoli. 'Come forward those of you who will take communion.'

On their way home Leo had to point out that it wasn't really the blood and body of Christ which they had consumed.

'But it was!' Natasha explained. 'That is the miracle of communion. That horrible old cloudberry vinegar, and those stale scraps of bread, Leo, they were transformed into the real thing by our faith and by our love. The miracle is called transubstantiation.'

'It certainly didn't taste like the real thing.'

'What?'

'And tell me something else, Natasha,' Leo said quite seriously. 'What you did to me this morning. Was that transubstantiation?'

Natasha shrieked. 'That was a Natasha special. And it was our secret, okay? I don't think you should mention it to Nikoli and the others.'

Leo looked baffled. 'If you insist.'

'I do. I do insist. If you want me to do it to you again.'

'I do. I do quite want you to do it again.'

And that evening, that Christmas evening after she had indeed done it to him again, she stroked his hair and said, 'It upset me today, to see so few people gathered together to celebrate the birth of our saviour. I know I shouldn't ask you, Leo. I've noticed that food has been a little scarcer these last few days, and it seems to me you already perform miracles. But those people stayed away today only because they are suffering so badly. I just wondered if there was any way we could help them.'

48

Leo lay with his eyes closed, glistening with sweat, recovering, considering Natasha's request. Truth was he had already decided upon a course of action. 'Tomorrow,' he said decisively, 'I will go out, and I will see what I can get.'

Natasha kissed him.

Fortified by some of Yevgeny's tea he went out the next day, to the Haymarket. The same unsavoury tangle of spivs were gathered there, dealing in patties and onions and wizened beetroots. Leo walked past the sparse stalls a few times. The fat spivs eyed him sourly, stamping their feet against the cold, snuggling into their furs.

Leo retreated from the scene, finding a bombed-out shell of a bakery where he could sit and gather his thoughts. An open oven gaped, as if in surprise and dismay at its sudden superannuation. The opium was strong and the umber-coloured Leningrad of mid-morning was filling up with antic staircases, along which dead boys ran and flitted from stairway to stairway like small birds in a gigantic aviary. Then the doppelgänger came clambering down one of the ghost staircases, wielding a spade.

'Where have you been? Haven't seen you in a while.'

The doppelgänger wasn't looking too good. He was suffering from scurvy, and his mouth was pustuled with a fresh outbreak of cold sores. His coat hung from his limbs in rags, and he had about him a gamy odour. 'What do you care? Are you going to wait about here all day or are you going to earn us a patty or two?'

Leo didn't answer. He felt nauseous.

'Well?'

'Don't rush me. I'll go in my own time.'

'Don't wait too long,' said the doppelgänger, disappearing further into the bombed-out building with his spade. 'I'll get started.'

Dispirited, Leo returned to the small circle of stall-holders. He sought out the furs-and-beetroot trader, who seemed to recognise him, and who thrust out that fat blue slug of a tongue. 'Looking for a sweet pattie, pretty rose?'

'No. I just want a few beetroots. And an onion if you've got any.'

The trader levitated his eyebrows in surprise, waggling them suggestively before nodding in the direction of a dark alley a few metres away.

'No,' Leo said. 'I don't want these others to see me go off with you. See that bombed-out bakery? Meet me up there in a few minutes.'

'If you insist, pretty rose.'

'And please bring my onion.'

Leo dragged himself to the appointed place. It was a long walk, and the dirty compacted snow squeaked under his feet. He had to pass a burned-out tram car, its twisted, rusting frame like the skeleton of some fantastic beast. He took up position in the shadows of the bakery. Hiding in the oven, the doppelgänger flashed a shard of mirror at him in signal of readiness.

*

'It's not that they're not grateful,' Natasha cooed in his ear. 'It's just that they keep asking me how you do it. None of them have seen a beetroot or an onion in months, let alone all this. And such a wonderful stew! They keep asking me and what should I tell them?'

Leo had instructed Nikoli to gather together the underground faithful, particularly those who were hungry and suffering. He'd specified that they should bring a vessel, and that he would feed them. A congregation larger than usual turned out and Nikoli had conducted his candlelit service, after which Leo produced a vat of stew, dispensing equal and generous measures to everyone. He was disappointed that Nikoli hadn't incorporated this apportionment into the service, but he said nothing.

Natasha was insistent. 'They're all saying you work miracles, Leo.'

'It's not miracles.'

'But what shall I say to them when they ask what it is they're eating?'

'Say, "Best steak!" and don't wink.'

'I can't keep doing that! It's wearing thin.'

Leo dragged her aside and whispered harshly, 'What do you want to tell them? That what they're stuffing into their mouths is a putrid and decomposing rat chopped up with one of last year's beetroots? Tell them. Go on. See how that salts it for them.'

But Natasha had savoured rattus norvegicus more than once in the days before Leo stumbled into her life. She

51

knew all its culinary limitations. 'Don't be angry, Leo. You work wonders. Everybody says so.'

But Natasha couldn't let the matter drop. The problem was that she was a true economist. It wasn't the Communist Party re-education camps who had imparted to her the universal laws governing the distribution, exchange and consumption of goods or the principles of surplus value; it was her career as a prostitute. Whoredom was a schooling based not on the classical laws of Diminishing Returns, but on the neoclassical tradition of Marginal Utility. Put another way, she knew the price of a fuck, and from that principle, asserted the neoclassical school of Whoring Economics, it was possible to calculate the price of everything.

Watching Leo dose himself with the dwindling resource of Uncle Yevgeny's tea made her think of her sisters of commerce fortifying themselves with vodka before an evening's work. It had crossed her mind several times that Leo was going out and whoring himself, but she knew that even the Tsar's courtesans couldn't have done this well in such conditions. So, swathing Isaac in blankets, she resolved one day to follow Leo.

The uncertain hour of The Whistling Shell was always Leo's favourite time for a foray, and at whatever time it came. Just like the underground Christian circle, his activities were protected by enemy fire. The sound of the first soft hooting of shells was to him like a peal of bells or the call of the adhan, and on this day the German bombardiers wound their timepieces for a noon invocation of the Kruppsteel God. With shells detonating about the city he went out, evidently without fear. She followed his slightly unsteady gait as he trudged the blackened snow along the street in the direction of the Haymarket.

He had no idea she was following him. He never looked back. Indeed, he seemed oblivious even to the bombardment going on, and instead of turning his head in the direction of this or that explosion, his eyes seemed to move up and down the vertical structures of the tallest Leningrad buildings, as if tracking someone moving among the parapets and the rooftops. Natasha's heart squeezed for him, this tender, distracted boy. At that point she almost went home, knowing from experience and intuition that she might find something here that would destroy their precarious and singular time together. He'd already delivered her from a world where no one asked another's business, where one learned to look the other way, where one remembered to forget instantly; and not because the truth couldn't be guessed at, but because it could. But she didn't turn back. He was too much of an enigma, this Leo, and she had to find out where he went.

Squeezing Isaac tight to her chest, Natasha followed him across the city for half an hour, until he reached the Haymarket. She had to duck into a doorway when, for the first time, he glanced around furtively. He didn't see her, she was certain, and she was more careful when she followed him into the charred wood and twisted steel wreckage of an old bakery.

Loitering behind a blackened pillar she watched him

uncover a spade. He began scraping at the snow, but what puzzled Natasha was the argument he conducted with some unseen person. The dispute was acrimonious, and Natasha peered round her charred pillar to look for Leo's adversary, but she could see no one. Her heart quickened when she realised Leo was in dispute with none other than himself.

Leo remonstrated bitterly, working all the while, chipping with his spade at the hard-packed ice. After a while he tossed away the spade and produced a small hacksaw from his pocket, applying it energetically to some object buried in the ground. Leo cut a leathery slice free of the packed snow and rammed it into his coat pocket before returning to his hacksawing with renewed frenzy. Natasha crept up slowly behind him.

At first Natasha couldn't identify the object in the ground. Even when it became plain that it was a man, buried on his side in the snow, she wasn't able to reconcile the evidence of her eyes. The hacksaw was digging into the cadaver for a choice cut of rump. Natasha could see that the partially uncovered head wore, at the throat, a frayed ruff of dark and dirty ice.

At that moment Isaac chose to sneeze, and to let out a bleat of protest. Leo stopped sawing, and turned slowly. He tried to smile at Natasha, looking like a guilty child, wanting but failing to ingratiate.

Natasha sank to her knees. 'Is this how you saved us? Isaac and me? Is this how?'

Leo flicked his fringe from his eye. Natasha fell forward, her elbows in the snow, gagging without vomiting.

She let Isaac slip from her grasp, as if he was befouled. Leo went to collect him up.

'Don't touch him!' Natasha screamed. 'Don't you lay a finger on him!' She gathered up her child and staggered away, slipping on the ice, falling on one knee, scrambling to put a distance between herself and the abominable Leo. 'Don't come near us again! Don't you ever!'

The shellburst had ended. Leo slumped in the burned-out bakery, staring into the black maw of the brick oven. A slack line of dead electric cable hung over his head, suspended between the broken walls, and the doppel-gänger lay stretched comfortably along its length, hands clasped lightly behind his head. 'That's torn it,' said the doppelgänger.

'She hates me now.'

'You can do no good,' the doppelgänger said in Uncle Yevgeny's voice. 'Don't try to do good.'

'What will I do?'

'Survive. You must survive.'

'Go to hell,' Leo said, and the doppelgänger faded very slowly in the freezing air.

Leo stayed for a long time in the bombed-out bakery, amidst the charred wood and twisted metal, trying to puzzle things out. Perhaps Uncle Yevgeny and the dop-pelgänger were right, perhaps he should never have tried to do good. In doing good on a purely random basis, with no expectation of returned favour, he had attempted to act as an antidote to the random dispensations of The Whistling Shell. And for a while that had worked, and

55

he was happy. But then selfishness had crept in, along with vanity and pride. When he had saved Natasha and Isaac from certain extinction, he had been too quick to gather up the rewards available in Natasha's love and respect, and within the boundless joys nesting in the cries and the gurgles of baby Isaac. From those two, and in the potential happiness of those two, he had taken his own happiness, and that, he knew, was where he had made his mistake.

For he had stolen Natasha and Isaac from the hungry God of The Whistling Shell. He had saved souls he had no right to save. The Kruppsteel God of The Whistling Shell was an indifferent God, and had forgiven him once, for the soul of Natasha, and twice, for the soul of Isaac. And The Whistling Shell had even fed him and those around him, had it not? But what The Whistling Shell could not forgive was desertion into the arms of another God, the jealous and cannibalistic God of the Christians. The feeding of the followers of this other God had made the God of The Whistling Shell angry. How could Leo ever make things right again? How could he ever restore faith?

As Leo brooded in that dark and icy place, the German gunners slipped in one of their random bursts of fire. Leo heard the single shell whistling softly, so softly it seemed to describe an illumined arc on its long trajectory through the freezing sky. Leo heard the whistle falter, waiting for the crump of explosion. But the shell, having landed, had failed to detonate. Instead it left an eerie silence, almost a vacuum, which was filled with whispered words. 'Give me Isaac,' it said. 'Your only son.'

Leo returned to his house. Natasha and Isaac were not there. The house echoed in their absence. Natasha had taken nothing which did not belong to her. All of the gifts of his mother's clothes and jewellery which Leo had made to her remained in the house. So too did Yevgeny's army-issue Bible, bookmarked by Natasha no deeper than a page of Genesis.

Leo waited three days for Natasha to come home. On the third night, dithering until the hour before dawn, he went back to look in the hideous apartment where he'd first found her. Silently he ascended the broken stairway, creeping into the room. She was there, lying on the bed under rank, coarse blankets, sleeping heavily. A muscular figure lay next to her, snoring. A sailor's cap hung on a nail on the wall. In a crib made in a chest of drawers, Isaac was awake. The baby seemed content, kicking his arms and legs. He gurgled happily as Leo lifted him out of the improvised crib.

Careful not to disturb the sleepers, Leo crossed the room without a sound, taking the baby with him.

Dawn was breaking, pearly-grey and tea-brown, as he walked through the streets clutching Isaac to his chest. Before he'd walked a quarter mile, he heard the first salvo of a German wake-up call. The shell was still whistling, this morning with a slight trill as its fins baffled the air currents, as Leo looked up saying, 'O thank you. I knew you would come.'

The first shell exploded somewhere near the Admiralty tower, followed by a series of muffled reports in the same vicinity. Leo made his way to Uprising Square and along

Nevsky Prospect, hurrying towards the thick of the bombardment. A pale winter sun was climbing to the east of the Admiralty tower, flaring on the debris kicked up by the shell blasts, making dust fountains and ragged sculptures of floating ash. One building that had already taken a hit in a previous bombardment was on fire. Shells rained down ahead, some exploding, others failing to detonate in the deserted street. It seemed to him that more and more of the German shells were failing the longer the campaign went on. Leo saw another three shells blast the front house of the old cinema. That being the place where the shells rained thickest, he crossed the street and carefully placed Isaac on the icy pavement outside the burning cinema. He himself sat cross-legged on the dirty ice, and waited.

The barrage abated for a while, before resuming with increased ferocity, raining shells around them. Two buildings took direct hits; shards of scorching shrapnel went smoking and skidding across the icy road, but the main bombardment moved across Nevsky Prospect and settled at a distance of forty or fifty metres removed. Leo swept up Isaac and scurried towards the new target of the shells. One round came whistling in, thumping the elevation ten feet above his head, embedding itself in the concrete without detonating, the fins of the shell protruding from the wall like a cathedral gargoyle.

Neither he nor Isaac received so much as a scratch.

Again the locus of the barrage shifted, moving back across the road and up Nevsky Prospect towards the tower. Leo was furious. With buildings burning around him he ran into the smoke and dust fountains, his face blackened with soot, screaming at the metal storm, 'Here we are! Take him back! You can take him back!' His tears smudged on the soot of his face. 'Why don't you take the both of us?' he raged. 'Why won't you take us?'

But the bombardment shifted several degrees west of their position, and then the volleys ceased, quite suddenly. The only sound was of fires crackling and smouldering about him, and of dust and ash resettling on the ice pavements. He stood in the middle of Nevsky Prospect, hanging his head, and he knew it was over.

He knew it was over for everything: for God; for Communism; and for the smooth deity of The Whistling Shell. He knew now that The Whistling Shell in all its savage indifference didn't want Isaac back. Neither Isaac, nor Natasha, nor him in place of any of them. The Whistling Shell wasn't counting the corpses. It wasn't in the business of claiming souls, or balancing endless figures in infinite ledgers. The truth in this was quite horrendous. It meant that you could do good, and you could do bad, and even that you could try to do good by doing bad; but that nothing and no one could praise you or forgive you, but yourself.

It meant only this: that the purpose of a good life was a good life, and nothing more, nor less.

And as the smoke of bombardment cleared he looked about him and the innumerable staircases and ladders and flights of steps and platforms were diminishing, fading, closing down. The old Leningrad, the one from which he'd emerged, was reasserting itself.

It was a long walk back. People emerged from their houses to survey the latest damage. Men and women who would not be surprised by anything to be witnessed in the streets of Leningrad stopped to look at the ragged boy, tears streaming along his blackened cheeks, bearing in his arms a small baby.

He found Natasha in the streets near her hovel, who with Nikoli and some of the underground worshippers had come out to look for Leo. Natasha ran up and snatched Isaac from his arms, breathing a prayer of thanks that the child was unharmed. Nikoli stretched out a hand and touched Leo on the shoulder. The boy seemed not to see the old man.

'Does anyone know,' Leo said, 'the way to the front line?'

Natasha stepped forward, more than a little afraid of him. He didn't seem to recognise her. 'Leo, come back to us. I forgive you.'

'But can I forgive myself?'

'Whatever you have done,' said Nikoli, 'it can be addressed in Heaven.'

'You're wrong,' Leo said.

'Where are you going?' Natasha asked. 'What will you do?'

'It's time I got myself a gun. It's time I did the manly thing, and killed some Germans.'

They merely stared after Leo as he made his way out of the city, a small huddle of them watching in silence, with the sun turning a pallid yellow in the winter sky over Leningrad.

The fate of Leo Shapoval from that moment on is uncertain, though three stories circulate. One claims that he fought heroically in the lines, quickly becoming a young captain and from there, after changing his name, developed a career in the Communist Party. Another version suggested that he lasted mere days on the lines, and it was while recklessly leading a charge on the German lines that he was cut into a million pieces by the enemy machine guns. A third version insists that he survived the campaign and left the country in the confusion of the immediate post-war years, returning as a dissident, and that he was one of the architects of the overthrow of the Iron Curtain regime, dedicated to the renaming of his old city under a new administration.

I like to think the last version is true. Perhaps I want to think well of him, because, not knowing who my real father was, I think of him, Leo Shapoval, as my true father. He did after all give me life. And I only have the version of him told to me by my mother, his lover, Natasha. That and a photograph of Leo, taken before he had even met my mother, in which a young boy, perhaps a little too fat for his own good, smiles shyly into the camera, with no knowledge of the horrors foreshadowing him; and in which a strange and somewhat poetic curl of the lip seems to say to me across the years, 'What must you do? You must survive.'

How The Other Half Lives

'Like Lovegrove's novels *The Hope and Days, How The Other Half Lives* (and what a cunning title that turns out to be) describes a monstrous edifice founded on injustice. There is a stealth in its calm; there is a courage and anger in there that will make you blink and marvel.'   COLIN GREENLAND

'A highly enjoyable Faustian tale. Fast paced and with a surprising plot twist. A fabulous cautionary tale about greed and ego, proving once again that James Lovegrove has got what it takes to hit the big time'

MICHAEL ROWLEY, WATERSTONES

'A neat modern fable, elegantly told'   THE TIMES

'The story is developed with his usual wit and attention to detail and some excellent dialogue'

CHRIS GILMORE, INTERZONE

'The best and brightest from Britain's genre writers. A lavish feast . . . a gourmet treat'   THE TIMES

'Fiction that is blessed by the devil himself'

DAILY EXPRESS

'Superbly written'   STARBURST

'A good example of what is best about the dark fantasy of century's end'   DREAMWATCH

JAMES LOVEGROVE

How The Other Half
Lives

The right of James Lovegrove to be identified as
the author of this work has been asserted by him
in accordance with the Copyright, Designs and
Patents Act 1988.

This edition published in Great Britain in 2000 by
Millennium
An imprint of Victor Gollancz
Orion House, 5 Upper St Martin's Lane,
London WC2H 9EA

HOW THE OTHER HALF LIVES first published by Victor Gollancz in
2000 as part of FOURSIGHT, edited and with an introduction
by Peter Crowther

To receive information on the Millennium list, e-mail us at:
smy@orionbooks.co.uk

A CIP catalogue record for this book is
available from the British Library

ISBN 1 85798 759 7

Typeset by SetSystems Ltd, Saffron Walden, Essex
Printed in Great Britain by Clays Ltd, St Ives plc

One

It was another merely magnificent Monday in the life
of William Ian North.

The chauffeur picked him up from the mansion punc-
tually at seven fifteen a.m. and ferried him into the heart
of London within a purring Daimler cocoon. In the back
seat, North scanned the *FT* and checked the Nikkei Dow
closing figures on the in-car terminal. The stereo played
Wagner – operatic *Sturm und Drang* to get the heart
pumping, the blood racing.

Arriving at the NorthStar International Building at
eight thirty, North crossed the marble atrium and
acknowledged the salutes of the uniformed guards at the
security desk with a brisk nod. A private lift whisked him
up twenty floors to an office the size of a ballroom,
where a glass wall gave him a panoramic view of the
City, its domes and dominions, edifices and empires all
agleam in the new day's sun.

At his desk, whose calfskin-topped surface could have
easily accommodated a kingsize mattress, North officiated
all morning. He contacted various associates around the
world via audiovisual telelink. For some of the people he

1
.

was talking to, it was early evening; for others, the wee small hours of the morning. The time difference bothered neither him nor them. When William Ian North called you, it was at his convenience, not yours.

He brokered deals. He bought. He sold. He transferred from liquid to certificate and vice versa. He shifted between currencies. He invested. He disposed of. He topsliced and undercut. He creamed off and shored up. Across the planet, companies, industries, nations prospered or declined according to his dispensation. On a widescreen TV near his desk, tracker software registered the progress of the London market, describing the earth tremors of loss and gain as a wavering red line on a graph. The line seemed to respond to every one of North's decisions, every flex or contraction of his fiscal muscles.

He took lunch in the boardroom with a dozen of his immediate underlings. Business was not discussed, but every word North said, every nuance of every sentence he uttered, was listened to with the utmost attentiveness and later dissected and analysed, divined for hidden significance. As soon as the five-course meal concluded, one of the underlings was summoned to North's office and sacked for failing to meet her quotas. In truth, the woman had missed her mark by only the narrowest margin, but the occasional summary dismissal of an upper-echelon employee did wonders for the productivity of the rest of the workforce. 'It is thought well to kill an admiral from time to time,' as Voltaire said, 'to encourage the others.'

For half an hour North then rested, reclining supine on a velvet-upholstered chaise longue in a side-chamber of his office. Eyes closed, he sensed the thrum of activity emanating up from the building below. Beneath his back were a thousand people, each of them electronically connected to a thousand more, and all of them dedicated to a single task: that of augmenting the worldly wealth of William Ian North, inflating his already obscene capital value to yet greater heights of obscenity. He could feel them through layer upon layer of concrete and steel girder as they telephoned, tapped keyboards, made choices and calculations. For the most part he did not know their names; had no idea what they looked like. They were termites in a termitary, toiling frantically and anonymously on his behalf.

At three p.m. precisely, a staggeringly beautiful woman dressed in a crisp, short-skirted business suit was brought up to North's office by the chauffeur. This event occurred at the same hour every weekday. The woman was not always the same woman each time, but she was always unspeakably, apocalyptically gorgeous – in her field, the very best that money could afford. After the chauffeur made a discreet exit, the woman stripped bare and pleasured North on his desk. Then she dressed and departed, and North showered in his private bathroom, put on his suit again, along with a fresh shirt straight from the tailor's box, and resumed work.

By five, with the London market closed, North was ready to go home. Electronic memos had been squirted off to various foreign subsidiaries, giving advice on which

3

holdings to keep an eye on, which to get rid of if they fell below a certain threshold, which to acquire if they rose above. There had been a small blip with a Latin American asset, nothing major, a depreciation of a few million, a drop in the ocean. Nevertheless, North demanded that an investigation be made into the loss and the person responsible disciplined. Apart from this, he left his office content that everything was running smoothly with NorthStar International and would continue to run smoothly overnight until he returned the following morning to pick up the reins once more.

The chauffeur drove him out of the darkening city, through the streams of red taillights, westwards into the sunset and the dusk-cloaked countryside. North thumbed through the *Evening Standard* and listened to Elgar. The music stirred nothing more in him than a vague sense of yearning, a knee-jerk nostalgia for a pastoral, idyllic England that never was. The newspaper was gossipy, simply written, undemanding.

By six thirty he was back at the mansion again. The chauffeur bade him goodnight and steered the Daimler back down the driveway to the lodge, where he would wash, wax and vacuum the car in readiness for tomorrow, then have supper with his wife and go out to the pub.

The domestic staff were long gone. A gourmet supper awaited North in the kitchen refrigerator, needing only to be heated up in the oven. North stood in his mansion, alone.

No, not quite alone.

In his study, he took a key from a hook attached to the mantelshelf above the fireplace. The key was long, black, iron, old-fashioned, solid. Clenched in North's fist, its teeth poked out one side of his fingers, its oval turnplate the other.

With the key, North went over to one of the bookcases that lined the study walls and tweaked a leather-bound volume of Dumas. The bookcase swung inwards to reveal a short, dusty passageway. North entered.

The bookcase automatically eased itself shut behind him as he strode the length of the passageway. He could reopen it by pressing a lever mounted on the wall beside its hinge mechanism. Arriving at a heavy wooden door at the far end of the passageway, he flicked a light switch. No light came on in the passageway, but from the other side of the door there was a muffled cry. Inserting the key into the lock, North turned it. A tumbler clunked chunkily. North grasped the door handle and rotated it. The door opened.

A vile stench gushed out through the doorway to greet him – an almost-visible miasma of awful odours. Faeces. Urine. Unwashed body. Stale, overbreathed air. Damp. Mildew. Blood. Despair. North recoiled involuntarily. Though he encountered the smell every day, he had never grown accustomed to it. He probably never would.

Breathing through his mouth, he passed through the door, closed and locked it behind him, then ventured down a flight of stone steps.

The room was fifteen feet by fifteen feet by fifteen feet, a windowless subterranean cube. The walls were whitewashed brick, the floor just plain brick. Illumination came from a single unshaded lightbulb wreathed in cobwebs and controlled solely by the switch outside.

Once upon a time this cellar had been used for cold storage. Now, in one corner there was a thin mattress, little more than a pallet really, its ticking patterned with countless stains, stains overlaying stains like jumbled continents on a map of a destroyed world. Beside the mattress there was a chamberpot draped with a square of teacloth. Next to that there was a half-used candle in a saucer, a water canteen, and an empty enamelware dish.

In the opposite corner someone crouched.

He was still just recognisably a human being. Tattered clothing hung on him like castoffs on a scarecrow. Bare, blackened feet protruded from the cuffs of what had once been a pair of designer jeans; a filthy Armani shirt clad a torso as bony as a dishrack. He was covering his eyes and snivelling. His fingernails, like those of his toes, were long, splintered and brown. The dark, straggly, matted hair on his head meshed with his dark, straggly, matted beard in such a way that it was impossible to tell where one ended and the other began. Rocking to and fro, the man huddled in the corner, trying to make himself as small as possible.

'Well, good evening again,' said North.

The man moaned and pressed his hands more tightly over his eyes.

'Look at me.'

Slowly, with reluctant obedience, the man parted his

fingers slightly to form a lattice, through which he squinted up at North.

'Please,' he croaked.

'"Please"?' said North, tapping the door key up and down in his palm like a Victorian teacher with a ruler, sizing up a wayward pupil.

'Please don't,' said the man.

'Would that I had a choice,' said North, and, pocketing the key, stepped forwards.

The beating lasted five minutes. With the same imperious ruthlessness with which he pursued his financial affairs, North punched and kicked, slapped and struck, pounded and thumped. The man put up no resistance. The blows rained down, and he endured, crying out only when he was hit in a particularly tender spot, perhaps where an old contusion from a previous beating had not quite subsided or an old abrasion had not quite healed. He let the force of each impact knock him around wherever it would, rolling now this way, now that, making no effort to protect himself, for he knew that, whatever he did, North would always find a vulnerable area. If he tried to cover his belly, North would aim for his back; if he tried to shield his back, North would aim for his belly.

Eventually it ended, and North stepped away again, panting. There was blood on his knuckles, blood flecking his shoes. The man was coughing and gagging on the floor, writhing, fingers clawing at the slimy bricks.

'There we go,' said North, when he had got his breath back. He brushed his palms against each other. 'That's *that* over with for another day.' Tugging on his trousers creases, he squatted down so that his face was just a yard or so from the man's. 'You do understand how necessary all this is, don't you?'

Pink saliva bubbled between swollen lips.

'Look at me.'

North had been careful to stay clear of the man's eyes. They were the only part of him that he never hit.

The man's eyelids parted. Wincingly he peered up at his jailer and abuser.

North looked deep into his ice-blue irises. 'You *do* understand?' he insisted.

Painfully the man nodded.

North continued to gaze down on the man with his own ice-blue eyes. There was a long silence during which each beheld the other – the sharp, clean, expensively coiffed, smooth-shaven magnate and the unkempt, squalid, tangle-haired, mad-bearded prisoner. The face of one was tanned and flawless, the planes of its cheeks and chin well-delineated, its skin showing the evidence of weekly massaging and moisturising by a beautician; the face of the other was pallid, bruised, covered with sores, seamed with grime.

The moment of contact between the two men's matching eyes seemed to last for ever. Something passed between them, as it always did. Something that was like loathing but also like empathy.

Then North rose, and the man turned his head away.

North went to pick up the dish, canteen, and slopping chamberpot, and carried all three items up the steps. He unlocked and opened the door and went out, closing and locking the door behind him. A short while later he unlocked the door again and came back down with the chamberpot emptied out and wiped clean, the canteen refilled with water, and the dish laden with chunks of brown bread and cheese. The prisoner had not changed position in the interim. He was still sprawled on the floor, whimpering every now and then as various aches and agonies spasmed through him.

North set down the chamberpot, canteen and dish beside the mattress. Then he delved into his trouser pocket and produced a crimson-tipped universal match, which he placed in the candle's saucer.

'There,' he said. His voice was almost tender now. It was as if the violence of a few minutes earlier had drained him, purged him.

The man neither spoke nor moved. Quietly North withdrew from the room, closing the door one last time. Again, the key turned in the lock. A moment later the light clicked out and all was dark.

TWO

An hour passed before the man stirred himself. Laboriously, hissing with pain, he levered himself up onto all-fours and began shuffling across the floor. When he reached the wall, he followed it round, groping, until he came to the food and water. He ate and drank in darkness. He was permitted only one candle a week, so he used it sparingly. He didn't need its light to be able to put bread into his mouth or lift the canteen to his lips.

Mr North had loosened a tooth again, so the man was obliged to chew on one side of his mouth. He finished almost all of the bread, leaving some for later, and ate about half the cheese. Sated, he crawled onto the mattress, curled up and fell asleep.

He was awoken some immeasurable period of time later by a brief, feathery tickling on the tip of his nose. His injured body had stiffened up while he slept. To straighten out his limbs and sit up was exquisite, rusty torture.

Carefully he reached out for the candle, and when his fingers found it, he ran them down its length until they encountered the match. Noises, from the same origin as the tickling on his nose, had started nearby – tiny claws tick-tacking on the enamelware dish, and a soft nibbling. Taking the match, he touched its head to the wall and scraped downwards.

On the third attempt, the match ignited.

In the flare of its flame, a pair of small black eyes glinted briefly, vanishing as their owner scuttled away into the dark. The man brought the match across to the candle. At first the candle refused to catch, and he held the rapidly depleting match to the wick with mounting anxiety. Then, just as his fingertips were starting to singe, the flame suddenly doubled in size, and he snatched the match away and extinguished it with a shake. The candle guttered indecisively for a few seconds, then began to burn with a strong, steady glow.

He scanned the room.

The rat was hunkered at the foot of the steps, just its nose and eyes showing. The man whistled softly, and with slow, tentative steps the rat came out from its hiding place and crossed towards him. Reaching the edge of the dish, where one of the smaller pieces of cheese already showed the marks of gnawing, the rat hesitated, as though awaiting permission.

'Not so bold now I can see you, eh?' said the man. 'Go on, help yourself.'

The rat snatched up the partially eaten piece of cheese in its forepaws, then settled back on its haunches and whittled the cheese down with its teeth until there was nothing left.

The man broke off another piece of cheese and held it out. The rat took the morsel from his hand and ate it under his approving gaze.

A third piece of cheese went the same way, and a fourth, and then the rat, evidently having eaten its fill, began washing itself, running its forepaws back and forth over its face and whiskers, licking and preening its dark-grey fur industriously.

Smiling, the man watched the rat at its ablutions. When it was done, he reached towards it very slowly, so as not to startle it, and stroked its back. The rat submitted to the attention happily. The man rejoiced in the sleek, velvety feel of the creature's fur and the warmth of its skinny body, remembering the first time the rat had let him touch it. How many months ago that had been, he could not recall, but he could remember vividly the sense of triumph he had felt – and the sense of relief, for on several of his previous attempts to stroke the rat he had received a bitten finger. Now the rat, though still timid, trusted him. It was his friend.

The man petted the rat until the ache of keeping his bruised, battered arm extended became too great to bear. He sat back on the mattress and rested for a while, and the rat crouched patiently on the floor, waiting for the next ritual of their regular candlelit meetings to commence. After the feeding came the drawing.

The man picked up the spent match and broke off its head, then revolved the curved, carbonised stem between thumb and forefinger until he had sharpened it to a point. Holding his makeshift pencil in his right hand, he turned to the rat.

'What'll it be today?'

The rat bristled its eyebrows and whiskers, regarding the man inquisitively with its bright black eyes.

'How about a tree? Haven't attempted one of those in a while.'

The rat did not demur, so the man set to sketching a tree with the match on the whitewashed brickwork of the wall.

The man did not know a time when he had not been a prisoner in this underground cell. As far as he was aware, he had always been here. For innumerable, interminable years he had lived in darkness – darkness interrupted once every twenty-four hours by the sudden blinding glare of light that presaged a visit from Mr North and a beating. The limits of his existence were this room, and continually renewed pain, and permanent misery.

But there were memories . . .

The man knew of things he had never seen. He dreamed of them sometimes. He could summon images of them into his head whenever he wanted.

Things like a man and a woman who could only be his father and mother. Like a house where he had been born and which he had called home. Like a school, and parks, and a town, and townspeople. Like books and television and radio. Like cars and buses and trains. Like hills – green, deep, and undulating. Like seas – green, deep, and undulating. Like winter and summer, autumn and spring. Like the sun and the moon. Like clouds and stars.

All these he could remember, could conjure up in his mind's eye – their colours, their textures, their smells. He knew what it was like to go on holiday and have picnics on the beach. He knew what it was like to sit indoors on a rainy day and listen to a piano being played. He knew what it was like to endure lessons in a classroom while outdoors was heat and sunshine, boundless freedom just a pane of glass away. He knew what it was like to attend college and partake of the hedonistic, last-gasp pleasures of student life. He knew what it was like to travel to work on a commuter express, jammed in a rickety, racketing carriage alongside dozens of men and women dressed, like him, in business suits. He knew what it was like to play squash and golf and tennis with workplace superiors, observing all the tactful laws of intra-hierarchy sports, defeating his opponents if he could, but stopping short of humiliating them. He knew what it was like to sink into the arms and loins of a sexual partner. He knew what it was like to work at a desk alongside other desk-workers and harbour ambition, nurture powerful dreams of success. He knew all these things as though they were parts of his own life.

Yet how could that be? How could he have these recollections, these impressions, these sensations lodged in his mind when he had never once set foot outside this room? The paradox troubled him, and sometimes he wished he did not have the memories at all, could just flush them clean out of his brain. For without them he would have no idea what he had been deprived of. Would not have the extra torment of knowing there was an existence beyond this harsh, wretched existence.

The tree he had decided to draw was an oak. With quick, deft strokes he etched its outline, thinking of an afternoon spent lying in an oak's shade, staring up into the radial splendour of its branches and seeing the sun dazzling through a complexity of rippled-edged leaves, casting shadows upon shadows, a myriad flickering shades of green. He did his best to capture the memory and majesty of the tree on the wall, but the match-pencil had a limited lifespan. Its charcoal was soon worn away and he had to abandon the drawing before he could complete it to his full satisfaction. Perhaps a tree had been a little ambitious. Hitherto he had usually confined himself to simpler objects, man-made ones more often than not – a car, a house, a chair. He had had a go at a willow once, but the drooping fronds had proved to be too much detail for his finite artistic materials.

Still, he was pleased with his effort. The drawn tree was inarguably oak-like, even if it was plainer and cruder than he would have wished.

He turned to the rat.

It was on the rat's behalf that the man had started doing the drawings in the first place. Had the rat never entered the cellar and his life, he would probably have never devised this form of entertainment. It was for the rat's benefit that he had originally taken a dead match and, in a spirit of light-hearted experimentation, dashed off a quick sketch on the wall – a rough, cartoonish representation of a rat. And he would probably have never repeated the experiment if the rat had not appeared so fascinated both by the act of drawing and by the finished product. The diversion had thereafter become a habit. Indeed, now, if ever the man for some reason failed to provide the rat with a daily picture – if, for instance, he could not get the candle to light, or Mr North had hurt his drawing hand so badly that he could not hold the match – then the rat would become agitated and register an angry protest, either by squeaking vociferously and scurrying around the cellar for several hours so that the man was prevented from getting to sleep, or by depositing a turd prominently in the middle of his food dish. The drawings, it seemed, were a source of solace to both of them. The man took pleasure in realising on the wall one of the intangible images that crowded his brain, while the rat took pleasure in –

In what, exactly?

It was unclear. It was obvious, though, that the rat did take pleasure in the drawings. Perhaps it derived its pleasure from the man's pleasure, through a sort of interspecies emotional osmosis. The man was unwilling to question the phenomenon too closely in case the act of querying robbed it of its magic. He was content to accept that he and the rat shared some kind of unspoken bond, and leave it at that.

The rat was eyeing the oak with all the beady attentiveness of a professional rodent art-critic. All at once, it dashed over to the wall and reared up, supporting itself with its forelegs, to sniff the picture all over, from the apex of the tree to the base of its trunk. Then it leaned round to look at the man. Its whiskers were fibrillating madly, reflecting the candle's flame as a golden shimmer.

The man stared back, curious. The rat showed more keenness about some of his pictures than others, but usually it was depictions of smaller objects that excited it. The man assumed this to be because the rat lived in a rat-proportioned world, where things that were small to humans loomed large in its perception and things that were large to humans were altogether too massive for its mind to encompass. In this instance, however, the rat had become worked up about something that was, by its standards, unfathomably immense. The rat never sniffed a picture unless it liked it. If it was unenthusiastic or indifferent, it would merely sit still, perhaps nod its head up and down contemplatively, perhaps twitch its whiskers once or twice. Today's offering, it seemed, had earned

its artist full marks, ten out of ten, a big Double Glouces-
ter on the cheese scale.

'Well, thank you,' the man said to the rat, genuinely
gratified.

The rat sat back on its haunches, forepaws crossed, as
if to say the man was welcome.

The man rewarded the rat with an extra chunk of
cheese. Securing the chunk behind its incisors, the rat
departed. It scampered to a corner of the room where
there was a hole in the wall, a triangular fissure that
looked too small for anything bigger than a mouse to
crawl through. The rat glanced over its shoulder at the
man, then dived into the hole. It squeezed and squirmed
its way in until only its hindquarters remained visible.
Then, with a scramble and scurry of its back legs, it
shoved the last of itself through. A flicker of pink scaly
tail, and it was gone.

For several minutes the man stared at the hole, feeling,
as ever, a pang of parting-sorrow. He consoled himself
with the thought that the rat would be back tomorrow.
So, of course, would Mr North, but he preferred not to
think about that. He preferred to think about just the rat.

Wearily he turned back to the drawing of the oak tree.
He looked at it one final time, wondering what the rat
had thought so special about it, then took hold of the
cuff of his grimy shirt and wiped the picture off the wall
with his sleeve, rubbing and rubbing at the spot until
every last trace of charcoal had been smeared away. He
had known instinctively, from the day he drew that very
first picture for the rat, that Mr North would not approve

of finding drawings on the wall. Mr North would consider such a thing a dangerous indulgence and, in order
to compensate for it, would have to beat him harder. He
might even take the candle away, in punishment. Thus
the drawings, like the rat, had to remain a secret from
Mr North.

The man ate the rest of the bread, then licked the tips
of his thumb and forefinger and pinched the candle out.

In the darkness, he stretched himself out on the mattress once more, gritting his teeth and gasping at the
twinges and the throbs and the dull, dolorous aches that
inhabited his body.

Soon, despite his pains, he was asleep again.

Three

It began as another typically titanic Tuesday in the life of
William Ian North.

The journey into London was mostly unproblematic.
Owing to roadworks and a faulty set of traffic lights,
North arrived at the NorthStar International Building a
few minutes later than usual, but the delay was negligi-
ble, and he was soon ensconced in his office and working
as normal, issuing edicts and directives left, right and
centre to associates and subordinates both within the
building and overseas. The London market was having
an unsettled morning, fluctuating a little more violently
than was desirable, but with North's assistance its trend
remained upward.

Lunch was enjoyable, apart from one minor mishap. Smoked salmon was served as one of the starter courses, and North had expressly stipulated that this should never happen. He did not dislike the taste of smoked salmon, but it was a food the poor ate when they were pretending to be rich, and North wanted no part of common, cheap extravagances. A sous-chef was given his papers and shown the door.

North rested well after lunch, and was serviced admirably by his three o'clock prostitute. The woman was not perhaps his favourite among the professionals who regularly visited him, but by any objective standards of pulchritude she was still indisputably, outstandingly ravishing. An élite-class woman, one far beyond the reach of ordinary men – or ordinary millionaires, for that matter. A billionaires-only babe.

Following his shower, North took his seat again at his desk and assessed how his assets had been faring over the past couple of hours.

He was shocked to discover that yesterday's Latin American loss turned out to be far more severe than had originally been estimated. It wasn't simply a matter of a few million any more. It was a matter of a few *hundred* million. As a consequence, several local lending banks had collapsed, a number of major corporations had gone under, and the ensuing economic devastation had led to the military overthrow of at least two recently established and precariously balanced democratic governments.

All in the space of a few hours.

North demanded explanations. They were hesitantly

forthcoming. From apologetic and sometimes trembling
directors, vice-presidents, chairmen and chief executive
officers he learned that the economic situation in the
region had been unstable for some while now – more
unstable than certain individuals had been prepared to
admit. Balance-of-payment deficits had skyrocketed. Bad
loans had been called in, and the debtors found incapable
of repaying. Minor problems that had been brewing for a
while had suddenly come to a head at once. It was as if
several snowballs rolling downhill, slowly gathering
speed and size, had unexpectedly converged and started
an avalanche. Things had happened too fast. The problem had developed into a crisis too rapidly to be averted.

North listened, fired the appropriate people, promoted
others, and spent the rest of the afternoon in a flurry of
fund-transfers, sell-outs and buy-ins, moving around
sums of money as vast as tectonic plates. By close of
business in London, he had the situation back under
control. Clicking the widescreen TV to a satellite news
channel, he saw that the military juntas that had deposed
the democratic governments had themselves been
deposed and the originally elected officials – those who
had not been shot – reinstated. Order had been restored.
NorthStar International itself had sustained a severe
financial blow, but North was confident that the loss
would be recouped within a few days.

He left the office in a grim mood that neither Elgar nor
the *Evening Standard* could alleviate.

The beating he delivered to the man in his cellar was
twice as brutal as usual and lasted twice as long. This was

not solely because North needed an outlet for his frustration, although that played a part. Principally it was because the increased viciousness would ensure that a day like today would not be repeated. It seemed that he had been going soft on his prisoner. He was not sure how this was possible, since he was not aware of treating the man any more kindly than usual over the past few weeks. Perhaps he had been slackening off with the beatings – pulling his punches, terminating the punishment after an increasingly short period of time – without realising it. And perhaps, incrementally and imperceptibly, he had begun putting more food on the man's dish. He would have to be more careful in future. It was vital that the man's sufferings were constant and unrelenting. Dr Totleben had been quite insistent about that. North must give the man no quarter, show him no mercy. To exhibit – even to feel – compassion towards him was to invite negative repercussions. The man must know no happiness, no delight, no joy. Ever.

North left the man with half as much food as yesterday. It was a very long time before the man was able even to think about crawling towards the dish, and when he did manage to reach it he found that his jaw was so pummelled and swollen that it would scarcely move. He was forced to eat the bread and cheese crumb by crumb, poking each piece between his lips and pushing it to the back of his mouth with his tongue. His body hurt too much to sleep, so he lit the candle straight after his meal and waited for the rat to come.

When it arrived, the rat was carrying something in its

mouth. It approached the man in a gingerly fashion, like a religious supplicant bringing an offering before his god. It dropped the object at the man's feet and took a few hurried steps backward.

The man, puzzled by this unexpected development, struggled to bend towards to the object and then bring it into focus with his pain-wracked vision.

It was small and ovoid, composed of two distinct sections, the one yellow-green and smooth, the other light brown and rough-textured, culminating in a short stem.

The rat helped itself to some cheese while the man strove to recall what the object was and what it was called.

At last the answer came to him.

An acorn.

Four

The man studied the acorn for several minutes, turning it over and over with trembling fingers. He was no longer aware of his pain. His attention was fixed on the acorn to the exclusion of all else. He stroked it; sniffed it; even stuck out the tip of his tongue and tasted it. He thought he could detect warmth within it – a lingering trace of absorbed sunshine? Was it summer outside? The temperature in the cellar never varied. Down here, it was always damp January.

He marvelled at the glossiness of the acorn itself, and at the dimpled surface of its cup, and at the tight precision with which the one fitted into the other. It was quite the most beautiful thing he had ever set eyes on. In it, he saw the outside world encapsulated in miniature. He thought of all that the acorn had experienced in its short, budding life. The elements had touched it. Rain had drenched it, wind had buffeted it, sun had beaten down on it. And people. People had looked at it. People who were not confined as he was. Fortunate, free-roaming people. They might not have actually noticed the acorn, but it had fallen within the scope of their gazes. Perhaps some of them had lain within the shade of the tree from which it had come. Perhaps children had climbed that tree, shinning their way up its trunk, straddling its branches, clambering –

His imagination, in full flow, suddenly froze.

The tree from which it had come.

He turned to peer at the rat, which, having gorged itself, was now enjoying its customary post-prandial clean-up. Sensing his scrutiny, the rat threw a brief glance his way, then resumed washing.

The man's head hurt to shake, but he shook it nonetheless. No, it wasn't possible. It was a coincidence, that was all. The rat was intelligent, but not *that* intelligent. No, this was what had happened: for reasons of its own, the rat had decided to bring him a gift. The acorn was a tribute, the rat's way of thanking him for all the cheese and the drawings. He should infer nothing more from

23

the event than that. The fact that the gift was directly
related to the picture he had drawn yesterday was of no
consequence. None whatsoever.

And yet . . .

He remembered how the picture of the oak had excited
the rat, despite the fact that the rat traditionally showed
little appreciation for drawings of large things. Was it
conceivable that the rat had brought him the acorn in
order to show that it knew that he had drawn an oak?
Was it trying to demonstrate that it was even smarter
than he already thought?

If that was the case, why had it not done so before?
Why had it waited till now?

Perhaps because, before now, he had not drawn anything that the rat could easily fetch evidence of. After all,
there was a limit to what the rat was capable of bringing
into the cellar. Anything that could not fit through the
fissure in the corner was excluded. Perhaps the oak was
the first picture he had drawn that the rat had been able
to act on in this way.

He tried to recall what else he had sketched for the rat
over the past few months. He had done so many pictures
for it, a couple of hundred at least. He could barely
remember a tenth of them. He knew he had drawn a
sailing ship once; the rat hadn't liked it. He had drawn a
book; that, the rat had seemed mildly interested in. He
had drawn a fanned hand of playing cards; that, the rat
had given its full, close-sniffing approval. He had drawn
a mountain; the rat had simply shrugged. He had drawn
an apple – yes, now *there* was something the rat could

have brought him a piece of. And, as he recalled, the picture of the apple *had* gone down well with the rat. And what about the willow? He had a feeling the rat had been reasonably intrigued by it. Surely, if the rat had wanted to show that it knew what a willow was, it could have presented him with a catkin the following day, or a leaf.

Yes. Maybe. But maybe the rat had not been able to locate an apple on that precise day. Perhaps the house above the cellar – the man knew that there was a house up there, and that it belonged to North – didn't contain any apples at that time. And perhaps the rat had not been able to find a willow, either, or had, but the timing had been wrong – when the man had drawn it, it had been winter and the trees had been bare.

So, all along, the rat had been waiting for a chance to prove himself. Each picture it had regarded as a kind of challenge. The man was asking it to retrieve these things from beyond the cellar, but until now it had been unable to comply successfully.

Was that it?

This would at least explain the correlation between the drawings and the degree of approval the rat accorded to each of them. The man had thought the rat preferred smaller things because it was familiar with them and had no understanding of objects over a certain size. But what if he had been looking at the situation the wrong way? What if the rat was gauging his pictures according to how easily it could obtain the item depicted (or a recog-nisable part thereof)?

It was incredible. Was a rat – a mere rodent – *really* capable of such complex mental processes? Could such reasoning and logic *really* be contained within that tiny, fur-capped skull? Surely not. Surely –

A sharp pricking on his left little toe interrupted the man's train of thought. He looked down to find that the rat sitting beside his foot, peering up expectantly. It had nipped him. It was waiting for him to do another drawing and had got bored and had nipped him!

'Cheeky little bugger,' the man mumbled with his barely mobile mouth. The words came out as *eegie igga ugga*. Had his damaged face allowed, he would have added a smile to the remark.

He picked up this evening's spent match and set about turning it into a drawing implement in the usual manner. Mr North had stamped on his right hand a couple of times during the beating, so the fingers were beginning to swell and weren't as dextrous as they might have been. Nevertheless, the man was determined not to be hampered by them. He was anxious to put his theory about the rat to the test.

What to draw? What to draw? Several times the match-pencil hovered over the wall, only to be snatched away before a mark could be made. What could he illustrate that the rat would be able to find? What was plentiful, perennial, common-or-garden, and could fit through the hole in the corner? He racked his brains. It was clear that the rat could come and go freely between the cellar and outdoors. Perhaps he should use this opportunity to find out whether it had the run of the house as well. Something domestic, then. Domestic and easily portable. Easily accessible, too. He didn't think the rat, clever though it was, was up to opening cupboards or drawers or undoing lids. A paper tissue, maybe? No, he doubted he had the draughtsmanship skills to represent one so that it was recognisable. A screw? No, people did not normally leave loose screws lying around. A paperclip? For the same reason, no. A flower? As a possibility, not without its merits. All the rat had to do was bring back a petal, after all. But really the man wanted something that was indisputably from inside the house. The rat might find flowers indoors, but it might equally venture outside for them. What about something from the kitchen, then? A tea-spoon? No, a teaspoon was an awkward shape and not easily appropriated.

What about something of Mr North's? Some small personal item such as a wristwatch. No, smaller than that. Something Mr North removed every night when he went to bed. Like a tie-pin or a cufflink.

A cufflink.

The man had had enough close-up experience of Mr North's fists to know that Mr North always wore cuff-links. The pair he most commonly wore consisted of flat hexagons of gold engraved with the initials W.I.N. More often than he cared to think, the man had glimpsed a flash of these cufflinks a millisecond before a punch connected.

What did you do with cufflinks when you undressed for bed? The man knew the answer to this question in the same way that he knew about everything else beyond the cellar walls – it was in his memories. He could see himself standing before a dressing-table, unpicking cufflinks from his shirtcuff buttonholes and laying them side-by-side in a small tortoiseshell tray. He was looking at himself in a mirror as he did this, admiring the immaculately maintained face and ice-blue eyes of his reflection, grinning serenely at himself.

Like all the man's other memories the image seemed to belong to someone else, yet at the same time he felt as though this *could* have been something he had done. It was as though he had fabricated a whole imaginary past for himself, and had somehow, over time, come to believe it might be real.

At any rate, he now had his subject-matter.

He roughed out one of the cufflinks, first the two hexagons, then the slender chain that joined them. He made the drawing large-scale – the cufflink as it might appear proportionate to him were he a rat. He suggested the shine of gold as best he could, using the cartoonist's shorthand of a small circle on each surface, denoting reflected light. Finally, he added the W.I.N. monogram to one of the hexagons, then leaned back to observe the rat's reaction.

The rat seemed unimpressed at first. Then – and the man was convinced he actually saw the light of recognition come on in its eyes – it sprang towards the picture and subjected it to a thorough, comprehensive, all-over sniffing. The creature was quivering from nose-tip to tail when it finally turned away from the drawing. It was almost as if it knew there had been a breakthrough; that at last the man had grasped what it had been trying to convey to him all these months. It darted off without a backward glance, plunging into the corner hole, a rat with a mission.

Candle snuffed, the man lay in the dark and counted all the many reasons why he should not expect the rat to return with the cufflink.

The cufflink had been an ambitious choice of object to be retrieved. Perhaps he should have thought of something simpler (although nothing simpler had sprung to mind). And then there was the possibility that the rat might not be able to gain access to Mr North's bedroom. And even if it could, it might not be able to reach the top of the dressing-table. And even if it managed that, the cufflink might not be there.

A whole series of even-ifs, each reducing the percentage chance of success that bit further.

And then, of course, there was the likelihood that the whole phenomenon was something he had invented. The rat was not some devastatingly brilliant master-rat but just an averagely intelligent rodent that could perform a couple of neat tricks.

But the rat had left the cellar with such apparent confidence . . .

Lying with the acorn clasped in his hand, staring into utter blackness, the man envisaged his little friend scurrying beneath the floorboards, behind wainscoting, up ladders of lath-and-plaster, through all the musty interstices of the house, searching for Mr North's bedroom.

Aloud, he wished it good luck.

'Oo uh,' was what he said.

Five

It was another wildly wonderful Wednesday in the life of William Ian North – for about the first five minutes of it.

Because five minutes was how long it took North to shave and start to get dressed, and it was as he started to get dressed that he noticed that one of his pair of gold monogrammed cufflinks was missing.

He rooted around in the tortoiseshell tray, stirring through all the other pairs of cufflinks there. The platinum pair. The ivory pair. The diamond-encrusted pair. The pair adorned with lapis lazuli Buddhas carved to a fantastically fine degree of intricacy. The pair made (allegedly) from the knucklebones of Howard Hughes. The pair fashioned from polished lunar olivine, so rare and irreplaceable that no insurance company would provide coverage for them.

The gold cufflink was definitely not there.

Had he been wearing the gold pair yesterday? No, yesterday it had been the turn of the platinum pair. He had worn the gold the day before, though, and remembered taking them off that evening. He could have dropped one then, he supposed. He checked beneath the dressing-table and, for good measure, under the bed. The cufflink was nowhere to be seen.

That left two options. Either the cufflink had been accidentally vacuumed up by a member of the domestic staff yesterday, or it had been stolen.

He discounted the latter possibility straight away. None of the domestic staff would dream of stealing something from the mansion of William Ian North, least of all an item as intimate and as readily missed as one of his cufflinks. None of them would be that stupid. They knew that not only would the culprit inevitably be found, but he or she would be *destroyed*.

North would phone his major domo once he got to the office and order a thorough search to be made for the cufflink. The household rubbish would have to be sifted. The whole building would have to be checked from top to bottom. If, after that, the cufflink still did not turn up, then measures would be taken. Inadvertent negligence was still negligence, after all. Someone's head would have to roll, and it would probably be the major domo's.

North was not a sentimental man. The gold cufflinks were significant to him insofar as they were the first decent pair he ever bought himself, back at the very beginning of his rise to moguldom. Nowadays, though, they were the most modest and least expensive pair he possessed. If one of them was lost for good, that was disappointing but no reason to get upset.

Still, the cufflink's disappearance annoyed him. Coming on the heels of yesterday's business traumas, it made him feel edgy and paranoid. Nothing was meant to go wrong. That was the bargain, wasn't it? That was what he had paid Dr Totleben all that money for. A life free from failure. Continued material success in everything he did.

Then he remembered Dr Totleben's words. He could see Totleben speaking them, see the little German as clearly as though he were standing in front of him right now – those quick, pecking nods of his bald head, his fingers plucking out trills on an invisible piano keyboard. 'But you understand, Herr North, it can never be always perfection, *ja*? The man for whom nothing bad ever happens, he is not a man at all, but God. You understand? And you, Herr North, are many things, but you will never be God.'

North was proud of his reply. 'Maybe not,' he had said, 'but will God ever be William Ian North?'

He donned the diamond-encrusted cufflinks, finished dressing, ate his breakfast, and by seven twelve was standing on the front doorstep, ready for the Daimler.

They encountered the first delay shortly after turning out of the driveway. For some reason – it never became clear why – a tailback had formed leading up to a normally unbusy junction. Still, there was the *FT* and the overture to *Die Meistersinger* to occupy North's mind, and the Daimler was soon past the hold-up and sweeping towards London at a fair lick.

The journey ground to a halt again on the motorway. A container lorry had jack-knifed across two lanes, and the rush-hour traffic was backed up for three and a half miles. As the car inched forwards, North resolutely ignored the gawping stares from drivers and passengers in vehicles alongside. You would think none of these people had seen an internationally famous tycoon in his Daimler before. He focused his attention on the Nikkei Dow figures as they scrolled across the screen of the in-car terminal.

Hang on a moment . . .

He pulled the terminal's keyboard towards him on its swivel-arm and tapped in a series of commands. Onscreen, certain holdings were highlighted, charts of their day's performance appearing alongside in inset windows.

What the . . .?

A rattling flurry of keystrokes.

'Quick, the phone.'

The chauffeur removed the car-phone handset from its dashmounted recharger and passed it over his shoulder to his boss.

North keyed a speed-dial preset number and held the phone to his ear.

No response.

He tried the number again.

Still no response.

'Bloody thing! Are you sure it's fully charged?'

Looking at North in the rearview mirror, the chauffeur nodded.

'Well, it's not bloody working!'

The chauffeur intimated that the signal might be blocked. Perhaps the exchange was overburdened – all the other businessmen in the cars around them trying to make phone-calls, too.

'But their calls aren't a tenth as important as mine!' North exclaimed, with perfect solipsistic logic.

He hurled the handset onto the footwell carpet and seized the terminal keyboard again. If he could not contact anyone in Tokyo, he would just have to manage things by himself from here.

The Far East was on the verge of meltdown. Certain key stocks had plummeted, dragging others down with them. Though trading on the Pacific Rim stock exchanges had ceased for the day, North knew that if he didn't act right now, the losses would continue when the exchanges reopened. Preventative steps had to be taken immediately, or the consequences would be catastrophic for NorthStar International.

Barely had he began to enter the relevant commands in the computer, however, than the screen image stuttered and jumped. A moment later, text began to disappear, to be replaced by jumbled nonsense – meaningless strings of numerals, punctuation marks, dingbats. Finally, before North's gaping, appalled eyes, the screen went blank.

He entered the key-sequence for Restart.

Nothing.

He switched the computer off and then on again.

Nothing.

He tried the if-all-else-fails tactic of hitting the machine.

The screen stayed stubbornly dead.

North screamed so loudly that the startled chauffeur nearly veered into an adjacent Bedford van.

'This can't be! This is impossible! It's a nightmare! This cannot be happening to *me*!' North continued to rant in this vein until they were clear of the jack-knifed lorry and were cruising at a respectable speed once more. At that point, he calmed down a little. They were making good progress again, and barring further obstacles he would be at his office soon, where matters could be taken firmly in hand.

Further obstacles presented themselves in the shape of roadworks (not just one set of them, as yesterday, but three), faulty traffic lights (affecting a major five-way intersection), and a bomb scare at the Bank of England, which brought most of the Square Mile to a standstill as police cordoned off streets and all the available alternative routes rapidly became clogged. The chauffeur used every back alley, cut-through and rat-run he knew, and even, at North's urging, drove the wrong way down a one-way thoroughfare, but for all his best efforts he was unable to get North anywhere near the NorthStar International Building until well past nine thirty.

North leapt out of the car when it was still a good half-mile from the building and ran the rest of the way. Sprinting through the entrance and across the atrium, he skidded to a halt at the doors to his private lift and hammered the call-button.

Nothing happened. No whirr of mechanism. The lift would not come.

He didn't bother hammering the button again. Obviously technology was against him today.

'The stairs!' he yelled at the security guards. 'Where
are the fucking stairs?'

A beefy index finger timorously pointed him in the
right direction.

Twenty flights up, a gasping, sweat-drenched, green-
gilled North staggered into his office and collapsed into
his chair.

The widescreen TV was showing a downward line as
steep as a ski-jump. His desktop telelink was, thank
Christ, operational. As soon as the fire in his lungs had
died down and he no longer felt he was going to vomit,
North set about addressing the situation in the Far East.

Again, as with Latin America, it transpired that numerous mini-crises had simultaneously ballooned into a
single maxi-crisis. Problems-in-waiting had developed
together into fully fledged problems, all exacerbating one
another – an exponentially cumulative concatenation of
shortfalls, implosions, disasters and depressions. Already
there had been eleven ritual suicides among the senior
management of NorthStar International's Pacific Rim
empire, and every face that appeared on North's screen
was glazed with tears and contorted with agonies of
contrition. But North did not want to hear regrets and
excuses. He wanted to hear strategies. For two hours
solid he and Asian underlings worked out a package of
countermeasures that would limit the damage to
NorthStar International's holdings in the region and
ensure a swift bounce-back. During this time another
three of his employees took their own lives, one of them
while North had put him on hold in order to talk to

someone else – the man simply got up from his desk, opened the window of his eighth-storey office, and stepped out.

By the time the countermeasures had been decided upon and implemented, North was a haggard, febrile wreck. He began putting together a projected estimate of the total capital devaluation NorthStar International was going to incur as a result of everything that had gone wrong today and yesterday, and stopped when the figure exceeded the available space on his calculator's readout. At least London seemed to be recovering. The ski-jump now ended in an optimistic little upturn.

Bad news from Russia swept in like a chill wind from the Volga. A *putsch* had occurred in Moscow. All western-owned assets had been seized and declared property of the state by the Communist/military axis that now held sway in the Kremlin. The country was in upheaval. Every one of his Russian employees North tried to contact either was not at his desk at all, or was lying under it, vodka bottle in hand, singing 'Kalinka'.

There was only one thing North could do. He called every western head of state currently on his payroll and decreed that political pressure be brought to bear on Russia. Embargoes, sanctions, blockades and even war should be threatened.

War *was* threatened. For half an hour the world tee-tered on the brink. Then, reluctantly and with much grumbling, the Communist-military axis backed down and agreed to return westerners' assets to their rightful owners. London surged back up to its start-of-day level, buoyed largely by relief that Armageddon had been avoided. Wall Street opened with a plunge, as if to indicate that it, too, had feelings, but then swiftly rallied.

Lunch? North barely had any appetite for lunch. Besides, not only was smoked salmon served *again*, but another proscribed dish somehow found its way onto the menu as well: roast pigeon, which North detested both because the meat was stringy, tough and tasteless, and because he could not disassociate the thing on his plate from a mental image of London pigeons with their frayed feathers and scrawny necks, gobbling up garbage and shitting all over the shop. North strode from the board-room spitting with rage. The kitchen staff were subjected to a volcanic tirade. Inexcusable! Unforgivable! Unacceptable! Outrageous! Sackings were meted out indiscriminately, like sparks shooting from a fire.

Dizzy with his own anger, North returned to his office and paged his personal assistant.

'Get me Dr Totleben,' he told her.

Three minutes later his PA came back with the news that Dr Totleben was away from his office, attending some kind of convention in Düsseldorf as Guest of Honour.

'No, you misunderstood me,' said North. 'When I said, "Get me Dr Totleben", I didn't mean get him on the phone, I meant *get* him. Send over the Lear jet for him. I want him in my office as soon as is humanly possible.'

He tried to rest, but he couldn't rest. The chaise longue felt lumpy and unwelcoming. He paced and paced and paced. His stomach felt like a knot of eels. It was drizzling over the City. The overcast sky looked so heavy, he thought it might give way under its own weight.

I was promised I could not fail, he thought. Totleben all but guaranteed it. Never mind what he said about my not being God. He was just covering his own backside, allowing himself a get-out clause. He told me nothing could go wrong, and today *everything* has gone wrong. There'd better be a damned good explanation, that's all I can say. A *damned* good explanation.

When his three o'clock whore came, he was tempted to send her away, but then thought that he could do with the distraction. Right now, perhaps a spot of mindless carnal abandon would be just what the doctor ordered.

The woman – incandescently lovely, but wearing a perfume that North found eye-watering and bitter – took her clothes off and his, and straddled him on the desk. North lay there, waiting for the flood of heat to his groin. The woman began to ride and fondle and wriggle. Ah yes, North thought, *this* is what I need. She explored his body with an expert touch. Lips, hands, vulva. Any minute now, thought North, the stress and strain of the morning will be nothing but a memory. All anxieties will have disappeared, subsumed beneath a tsunami of sexual pleasure. Oh yes. Any minute now. Forget the Far East. Forget Russia. Become lost in unfurling lust . . .

Limp as a paraplegic's legs.

The woman did everything she could.

Limp as a lorry-flattened lugworm.

Tweaked, tickled, tongued, teased.

Limp as a lounge-lizard's languor.

Rimmed, fingered, palpated, throated.

Nothing doing.

At last North threw her off and stalked over to the windows. Stark naked, he gazed out over the City, his ice-blue eyes glassier and more glacial than they had been in a long time.

When he turned away from the windows again, the prostitute was no longer there. She had beaten a subtle and hasty retreat. North showered off and reclothed himself.

When he re-entered his office, Dr Totleben was standing by the desk.

North was overcome by an urge to go over and hug the little German, but settled for a brisk, forthright handshake.

'Dr Totleben, thank God you could come.'

Totleben pecked the air and ran off a little scale with his left hand. 'It was an order I had no choice but to obey,' he replied. 'When William Ian North summons, one either answers his call or forfeits all rights to be called sane.'

'Please, please, sit down.' North drew up a deep, buttoned-leather armchair. 'Would you like something to drink? Some refreshments?' Totleben, seating himself, declined. 'Nothing at all?'

'*Nein danke*. So, Herr North, what appears to be the problem? And why this urgency? Why was I dragged away from the Fifth Annual Metascientists' Symposium – in the middle of a most interesting lecture by the

University of Chicago's Professor MacGruder on the topic of Infernal Thermodynamics – and rushed over to London with such haste?'

'What appears to be the problem?' North echoed. 'Dr Totleben, have you not been watching the news?'

Totleben executed a pair of contrapuntal arpeggios, one ascending, the other descending. 'If you are referring to the nuclear war that nearly occurred this morning, it so happened that word of the crisis reached us at the symposium during a practical demonstration of micromancy. Immediately we ran the runes through the randomising software and divined from the results that events would turn out well, and the symposium continued on as normal. Other than that . . . well, in common with most metascientists I am of a somewhat unworldly disposition. I do not really keep abreast of current affairs.'

'So you know nothing about the financial turmoil there's been all across the world these past couple of days? You haven't heard about the chaos in Latin America and Asia and Russia?'

'I'm afraid not.' Totleben jabbed his nose forwards three times in quick succession. 'But this turmoil you mention, this chaos – it has affected NorthStar International badly, *ja*?'

'Very badly. You see before you a man who has been robbed of nearly a quarter of his wealth in the space of thirty-six hours.'

'If that is so, then I also see before me a man who, even three-quarters as rich as he once was, still has more

money than most people can even conceive of.' Totleben
capped the remark by stabbing out the circumflex climb-
and-fall of the opening phrase of the last movement of
Beethoven's *Ninth*.

'That, Doctor, is not the point. The point is, you
assured me I would have nothing but success.'

'Forgive me, Herr North, but I assured you – '

North interrupted him with a wave. 'Yes, yes, I
remember what you said. The gist of it was, though, that
as long as that thing in my cellar suffers, I would not
suffer at all. And look at me.' He gestured at himself. 'Is
this the face of a man who is not suffering?'

Totleben peered at North's face, and nodded. 'So what
do you need from me, Herr North?'

'I need to know what's to be done. I need to know
how I can prevent this shitstorm from getting any worse.'

'Very well. But before we go any further, I must
remind you, Herr North, as I told you all those years ago
when we first met: metascience is not an exact science.
If you want testable hypotheses and systematically repro-
ducible results, I am not the man to be talking to. My
field is the fusion of the tangible and the intangible. I,
and my colleagues, operate in the narrow margin where
what is known and what is sensed overlap; where physics
and fantasy, chemistry and alchemy, biology and belief
collide. It is, in every respect, a grey area. Within it,
nothing can be pinned down with absolute precision.
Nothing can be stated empirically.'

'I understand that.'

'I hope, for both our sakes, Herr North, that you do.

Now, tell me about the clone-golem. You have been regularly mistreating him?'

'Every day.'

'Starving him?'

'I feed him just enough so he doesn't die.'

'Beating him?'

'Religously.'

'Keeping from him all means of entertaining himself?'

'Unless he thinks bruises and bleeding are fun.'

'He has no hope of ever escaping his predicament?'

'He's given up even trying to try. In the early days he'd make the occasional bid for the door, but he's long since ceased to bother.'

'Hmmm,' said the doctor, running off some double-handed, triple-octave glissandos. His bald head gleamed like the six-point ball in snooker.

' "Hmmm"?' said North, his voice beginning to rise. 'That's it? That's the best you can offer? "Hmmm"? Dr Totleben, perhaps you are forgetting how much you owe me. You were an unknown dabbler when I first tracked you down all those years ago, working at various ill-paying odd jobs in order to finance your esoteric experiments. I'd heard about you and what you claimed you could do, and I funded you to the tune of Christ knows how much so that you could devote yourself full-time to your researches. You had nothing – *were* nothing – when I found you. You had no reputation, no respect, no renown. I created everything that you are now. I *made* you! If it wasn't for me, you wouldn't be junketing all over the world to conferences and conventions and symposia. Your textbooks would not be on the shelves of every university library. Your eccentric hobby wouldn't have become a world-wide, legitimate field of academic study. You'd still be a desperate little nonentity, festering away in a crumbling council high-rise in Baden-Baden!'

Totleben spread out some smooth major chords. 'Please, Herr North, do not think me ungrateful for your generous patronage. Please also believe me, however, when I say that, even without you, the disciplines to which I adhere would still have gained respectability eventually. Science and mysticism are forever growing closer, are they not? As science progresses and becomes more complex, so our minds have to take greater and greater leaps of faith and imagination in order to keep with each new theory that scientists come up with. Ultimately science and arcane belief will become indistinguishable from each other. There are those, indeed, who already consider science an occult art. I, then, have invented nothing new. All I have done is taken a step before the rest of mankind takes it. I will not deny that the worldly benefits have been welcome, but when all is said and done it is the pursuit of achievement that spurs me on, the furtherance of my researches. In that regard, your difficulties with the clone-golem concern me because they present me with a professional and intellectual challenge. So, allow me to think for a moment. Could there have been a contamination of the tissue sample I took from you?'

'Is that the answer?' North asked eagerly, surmising that if that was the case, then all Totleben had to do was take another tissue sample and manufacture another clone-golem.

'Please, Herr North. I am musing out loud, that is all.'

'Oh. Of course.'

'No,' said the doctor, in reply to his own question, 'the laboratory was purified and sealed to the highest clinical and magickal standards. Hermetic in both senses. Then the growing method itself? Perhaps a flaw in the incubation and incantation? No, not possible. The sigils were time-honoured, the protoplasmic growth-solution the very latest that biogenetics has to offer. I created the tetragrammata using only the very best and most reliable kabbalistic sources, working them around A, C, G and T, the initial letters of the four genetic nucleotide bases in DNA. The encoding was perfect. No, there is no way that the problem can lie within the creature himself. Then some outside influence, perhaps . . .?'

And so on and so forth in this manner the doctor ruminated, while his hands, seemingly of their own accord, executed variations on a theme, skirling through melodic permutations and changes of tempo and key. North knew he should leave Totleben to his musings and get back to work. NorthStar International desperately needed him at the helm. However, he could not bear to let Totleben out of his sight, and so he prowled the office in an agony of impotence, keeping an ear attuned to Totleben's voice in case its tone should suddenly alter to a triumphal note of *eureka*. His PA had put a hold on all incoming calls. Unguided, London wavered uncertainly, fluctuating within a ten-point band. Outside, the buildings and pavements of the City succumbed to a sudden sluice of rain.

At last the doctor seemed to come to a conclusion. He stopped talking, at any rate, and North snapped round, hoping for enlightenment, resolution, answers.

Totleben's expression was not encouraging.

'Well?'

'Ah, Herr North, as I told you at the beginning, meta-science is not an exact science. We are dealing with forces that some might say have a mind of their own.'

'Meaning?'

'In metascience we are not immune for the laws of nature. Not only that but we believe that *nothing* is immune from the laws of nature. Even your stock markets reflect the system of checks and balances that operate within ecologies, *nein*? So, allowing for that, we must see that, in your case, a great pressure has been exerted in one direction – namely your tremendous, world-beating success. We must also see, therefore, that in the interests of natural equilibrium an equal and opposite counterpressure must be brought into play at some stage, in order to redress the imbalance.'

'What are you saying? Am I going to lose *everything*?'

'Bear with me. When I created the clone-golem for you, I invested him with every part of your genetic make-up that was predisposed to failure. In effect, I sucked all the potential fallibility out of you and transferred it into your twin organism. The creature in your basement is the absolute antithesis of all that you have become. He is, to his marrow, every dream of yours that will be dashed, every project that will not come to fruition, every prize you grasp at but cannot reach.'

'Yes, yes, you told me all this at the time.'

'I restate these facts so that you may understand clearly. You were already successful when I first met you, but now your success has exceeded all my expectations. This has put an undue strain on the capacity of the clone-golem. Sooner or later, Herr North, something must give. The wheel must turn. Not even you, with all the wealth you have at your disposal, all the power and influence you wield, can prevent that. Sooner or later, nature will find a way of evening things out – assuming she has not begun to do so already.'

'But why' – North clutched the air – 'why didn't you tell me this before? Why did I have to wait till now to find this out?'

'Because, Herr North, metascience is not an exact – '

North took two steps towards Totleben, fists raised. 'Say that one more time, Doctor, and so help me I'll throttle the life out of you.'

Totleben twitched all over, then calmed himself. 'If you would permit me, Herr North – this aggression is unwise. I say so, not for my personal benefit, but with regard to the clone-golem. It would be regrettable were you, for some reason, to visit such fatal violence on the creature. Killing me would do you little harm. Killing the clone-golem, on the other hand . . .'

North stared at the doctor, then nodded slowly to himself and lowered his hands. Totleben had emphasised, right from the start, that the clone-golem must always be kept alive. Physically the clone-golem was more resilient than most human beings, capable of enduring a level of hardship and abuse that would destroy an ordinary mortal man. There were limits, however, to what even that creature of metascientific origin could endure, and Totleben had warned North to be careful not to overstep them. Were North to do so, the consequences would be terrible for him. All the negative energy that had been stored up in the clone-golem over the years would be released at once. 'Such a torrent of misfortune,' Totleben had said, 'I do not believe even you, Herr North, would be able to withstand.'

'Maybe,' said Totleben now, 'you would do well simply to accept that there are some things beyond your control, Herr North.'

'I can bring this planet to the edge of annihilation and pull it back again,' North replied matter-of-factly. 'There is nothing, Doctor, that I cannot control.'

Totleben, unconvinced, prodded out a hesitant version of the Funeral March, then said, 'Well. If that will be all?' He raised himself from the chair as though hauling his body up a flight of stairs with his chin.

'Yes, that will be all.'

'Good. Professor Levi of Haifa University is chairing a debate on Fractal Demonology this evening that I would be loath to miss.'

'What about payment for your services, Doctor?'

'No need.'

'I insist that you should be paid.'

'If it will make you feel better that money changes

hands, then by all means, go ahead. Whatever figure suits you. You have my bank account details.'

North extended his hand. 'Thank you, Dr Totleben.'

Totleben performed a curt bow as they shook hands. 'Not at all, Herr North. An honour to be of service.'

After Totleben was gone, North made a careful survey of the world economic situation, foresaw no further disturbances looming on the immediate horizon, and informed his PA that he would be taking the rest of the day off. The chauffeur was instructed to bring the car round, and North was soon wending his way homewards through the comparatively light mid-afternoon traffic.

At the mansion, he dismissed the domestic staff. It occurred to him, just as the last of them was leaving the building, that he had not discussed the cufflink with his major domo. It could wait till tomorrow, he decided. For now, there was something more important that needed to be done.

There were riding stables in the ground of the mansion. North had not actually ventured out on horseback in several years, but he kept a few mounts and paid for them to be groomed and exercised just in case the mood for a jaunt in the saddle should take him. In the same way, he paid for a private golf links in the grounds to be tended and maintained, and kept a golf pro on permanent retainer, just in case he should feel the urge for a quick round of eighteen holes.

Now, he went to the stables and fetched a riding crop. Armed with this, he headed for his study and the cellar.

Six

The man was in so much pain, he almost felt nothing at all. It was as if there was a level beyond which physical agony ceased to have any meaning. If he lay still, the pain at least remained at a constant. If he tried to move, it bloomed to indescribable proportions. He lost and regained consciousness so frequently that it became hard to grasp what consciousness *was* any more. In the end, he knew that he had been unconscious only because he knew that he had not been so aware of his pain for a while. Otherwise, he was simply exchanging one kind of disembodied blackness for another.

Time ebbed by. Dimly he remembered that the rat was due to visit at some point. He could not recall, with his pain-ravaged brain, why the arrival of the rat should be any more significant today than it had been on previous days. Something about gold? He could not reforge the connection between the rat and gold. Perhaps the rat had already been and gone, and he had missed it. Even if it came, Mr North had seen fit to provide him with neither food nor a match. So the rat might as well not come at all. There would be no meal today and no picture.

Spreadeagled prone on the floor, the man quietly wept. Tears poured from his eyes, mingling with the congealing blood on his face. Crying was something that did not figure in his memories at all – or at least, in his memories of adulthood. Childhood tears he could recall, the natural response to a barked shin or a parental ticking-off or a moment of intolerable frustration. But grown-up tears? There had been no excuse for them, no reason good enough to warrant them. He had cried in this cellar, many times, but in the life contained in his memories – that false life he had never lived – he had managed to develop such a control over his emotions that nothing, not even grief at his parents' funerals, could irrigate his eyes. He must be a hard man, he thought, this man whose past he shared. A hard and un-self-forgiving man. And for all his terribly agony he found himself pitying him. As salt-water spilled down his cheeks and onto the floor, he felt a strange sense of relief that at least *he* was able to feel sorry for himself.

The rat did come, eventually. He heard it skittering and scuttering about. He heard it clamber all over the enamelware dish, as if unable to believe that it was empty. Finally, he heard the rat come bounding over to him. Something small and metallic clinked to the floor in front of his face. He tried to move his right hand to grope for the offering, and groaned as fresh pain blasted through the muscles, sinews and fibres of his arm. The arm remained static, as though welded to the floor. The rat chittered irritably, but there was nothing the man could do. Mr North had beaten him for – how long? Half an hour? Longer? Fists, feet and that riding crop, striking him again and again until the blows had merged into a single thudding drumbeat without end. He could not recall when he had last endured an assault so severe.

The rat became increasingly peeved by the man's unresponsiveness and immobility. It scurried all over the

man's body. It stood on his head and shrilled in his ear.
It even nipped him on the toe again, although, of course,
the man barely noticed – it was just one more source of
pain amidst a myriad. Finally, after defecating right by
the man's nose, the rat departed in high dudgeon, and
the man was alone again in the cellar, a mind trapped
inside a body in torment.

Imperceptibly the hours passed and the pain began to
abate, receding from all over his body to a few keys areas
– a hand, a knee, the ribs, the kidneys, the testicles. A
snapped tooth drilled relentlessly into his skull. Two of
the fingers of his right hand felt bent and broken. His
back and shoulders were covered with lacerations, Mr
North having pulled up his shirt and whipped him
fiercely enough to break the skin. Now, it was no longer
impossible for the man to move, merely sheer hell. He
was able – though he nearly passed out several times
during the procedure – to bring his hand up and feel the
floor in front of his face for the object the rat had
deposited there. He found the rat's turd first, and ardu-
ously wiped off his fingers on the bricks before resuming
the painstaking (and pains-giving) search for the rat's
other offering.

He found it. Two hard, smooth hexagons of metal
linked by a short, delicate length of chain. Slowly it came
back to him what this was, what he had drawn for the
rat to fetch.

He laughed as best as his throbbing ribs and flayed
back would allow. He laughed, and then he cried again,

and then he cried and laughed together until the sobs and the chuckles were one and the same.

In the cold confines of his brick-walled world, the noise echoed and reverberated. It sounded as though there were a dozen prisoners present, all racked with tragic joy.

Seven

It was another thoroughly thunderous Thursday in the life of William Ian North. At least, so he hoped, as he woke to it at six thirty a.m., brought forth from slumber by his alarm clock's sleep-censoring bleep.

Nothing went awry during his washing, shaving and dressing. He performed each task with the air of a man expecting calamity to occur at any moment, but the basin did not collapse, the mirror did not fall on top of him, and none of his clothes ripped as he put them on. The cufflink was still absent, but then he had not thought it would just miraculously reappear on the dressing-table overnight. Shirtcuffs secured with Howard Hughes's knucklebones (allegedly), he ate his breakfast. The toaster did not explode, the milk had not gone off, the handle of the cafetière did not come loose as he poured it, the marmalade did not contain broken glass.

The chauffeur made his scheduled appearance at seven fifteen. No problems with the car. Engine running smoothly, phone fully operational, terminal online and reporting promising signs of a turnaround in the Far East. The journey was somewhat stop-start, but there was no repeat of yesterday's tailbacks and other traffic tribulations. Arrival at the NorthStar International Building was achieved in reasonably good time. The lift was functioning again.

The London market slowly rose, and so did the value of North's vast portfolio. Every gain, it seemed, was earned only with the greatest of effort. North felt as if he were swimming against a strong current, walking into a powerful wind. But he made headway, that was the main thing. Effortful though it was, he was going forward once more, not back.

His shoulder ached from using the riding crop yesterday. His knuckles hurt, too, so much so that he could barely straighten out his fingers. As the morning wore on, however, and no mishaps occurred, he became confident that these minor physical inconveniences were worthwhile. His tactic had paid off. All it had taken was one particularly intensive beating for the status quo to be restored. Dr Totleben had been proved wrong, and North thought he knew why. The doctor had bleated on about forces of nature, but had neglected to take into account the fact that William Ian North was himself a force of nature – a great, sweeping hurricane of drive and ambition and will.

Lunch was delicious, the menu error-free. North's underlings observed their boss's upbeat, confident demeanour and inferred that all was right again with the world. Their relief communicated itself to the workforce.

Productivity in the NorthStar International Building leapt.

North enjoyed the post-lunch rest he deserved, and his three o'clock prostitute brought him – after a few tentative false starts – to tumescence and thence to bucking, howling orgasm. The rest of the afternoon passed as though in a dream, and before he realised it North was heading home again, at a comfortable pace, with a crisp tabloid and Elgar to reassure him that everything was back in its rightful place.

The clone-golem submitted to his daily beating with scarcely a murmur. In a way, the man's abject passivity was disappointing. North had not realised how essential a part of the ritual the groans and cries and flinches of his victim were. It wasn't that North enjoyed inflicting pain. Rather, it was that the audible and visible responses to his efforts indicated that he was doing his job properly. He assumed that the clone-golem was not fully recuperated from the previous day's drubbing. He was doubtless also weak from lack of food. North swilled out the blood-pinkened urine from his chamberpot, put bread and cheese on his dish, and gave him – why not? – a match.

North went to bed and fell into a deep, just, contented and dreamless sleep.

Eight

His broken-fingered right hand was incapable of holding anything. With his left, he clumsily swept the match

down the wall. Once. Twice. Three times. The match did
not even spark. In his mind's eye he saw its crimson
head crumbling with each downstroke, dextrin-bonded
sulphur wearing away to raw wood. A fourth time. Still
the match would not ignite. He mumbled a prayer
through his mangled lips. Please. Please let there be light.

And, on the fifth attempt, there was light.

The candle illumined the cellar. The man did not pause
to inspect his injuries. A glimpse of bulbously bent middle
and index fingers was enough for him. He turned his
attention elsewhere.

The rat was sitting beside the food dish. It hadn't
touched the cheese. Its bright eyes seemed to be demand-
ing one thing from the man. A picture.

And have I got a picture for you, my little friend, the
man thought.

He made a pencil out of the match and held it up to
the wall in his left hand. The pose felt ungainly. The
distance from hand to wall seemed hard to judge. With
his first stroke he accidentally snapped off a couple of
precious millimetres of the carbonised wood. Carefully,
slowly, he persevered, etching out a shape. He kept it
simple, and though the end-product was shakily rendered, it was also immediately identifiable. The rat
seemed to think so, at any rate. No sooner had it looked
at the finished drawing than it was off.

The man scrubbed the picture from the wall. Then, by
the light of the candle, he took from his pocket the two
items the rat had so far brought him and visually examined them, one of them for the first time. He couldn't

decide which was the lovelier, the acorn or the cufflink. In the acorn, nature had created something of marvellously deceptive simplicity, the blueprint for an oak compressed into a nut no bigger than a thumb-tip. As for the cufflink, mankind had used its ingenuity and know-how to take a raw material like gold ore and refine something from it as beautiful as gold, and then transform that gold into an efficient and elegant sartorial accessory. There was an interchange there, of sorts, embodied in these two seemingly unconnected objects – a transfer of complexity. One was condensed potential, the other potential condensed.

He returned the acorn and the cufflink to his pocket and snuffed out the candle.

That night he barely felt his injuries at all.

Nine

It was another frankly fabulous Friday in the life of William Ian North. Throughout, however, North could not escape the feeling that its fabulousness was a sham, a charade, a convenient façade for something altogether more unwholesome. Everything went according to plan, everything fell out to his advantage as it was meant to, yet everything seemed to be happening too easily. The morning traffic seemed too clear, the reports from his subordinates seemed too positive, the lunch seemed too well planned and presented, his rest seemed somehow too relaxing, the prostitute seemed too enthusiastic and accommodating, the stock market seemed too obligingly responsive to his financial manoeuvres. It felt constantly as though someone was doing him a favour. A card-dealer was taking from the bottom of the deck to give him useful hands. A teacher was supplying him with all the answers to an upcoming exam. A tennis coach was going easy on him, lobbing him nothing but slow drop-shots. The day was not without its challenges, and he worked hard, but all along he could not shake the conviction that someone, somewhere, was stringing him along. That behind its mask of impartiality, fate was slyly smirking.

He put this impression down to fatigue. It had, by anyone's standards, been a traumatic week. Little wonder that he should be feeling underwhelmed and exhausted by its end. He would have a completely idle weekend, he decided. Lie in bed. Finally make time to watch the laserdiscs that had been sent to him by the various movie companies he owned. Take long baths, long walks. Generally have a break for a couple of days from the pressures and responsibilities of being William Ian North.

Outside the mansion, the chauffeur wished him good-night. North told him that his services would not be required this weekend, and the chauffeur tipped his cap gratefully.

North entered the house. He was tired, and was looking forward to pouring himself a glass of brandy and starting to unwind. But there was, of course, one last duty to be done.

In his study, he took the key from the hook on the mantelshelf, not noticing that one of the brass fire-implements on the hearth below was absent. He tugged on the Dumas and the bookcase swung inwards. With a yawn, he entered the short passageway, rolling his shoulders like a boxer limbering up on his way to the ring. At the far end of the passageway, he flipped the cellar light-switch and brought the key down to unlock the door.

He heard footsteps behind him – bare feet, running. He half turned in time to glimpse a shaggy, bestial-looking silhouette bearing down on him. Something throbbed through the air and struck him on the side of the head. He heard himself cry out, felt himself fall. As pain exploded through his skull, consciousness closed on itself like a flower at evening.

Ten

The man stood over the prone form of Mr North, panting. With the brass poker still aloft in his left hand, ready to deliver another blow if necessary, he nudged Mr North in the ribs with his toes. There was no response. He nudged him again, harder. Mr North was out cold. As planned.

Bending down, the man laid the poker aside and wrested the key from Mr North's fingers. He unlocked the door and opened it, then, stowing the key in the frayed breast pocket of his grubby shirt, he grabbed Mr

North by the armpits and set to hauling him through the doorway.

Mr North was by no means heavy, but to the man, debilitated by years of confinement and malnourishment, he weighed a ton. The pain from his broken fingers didn't help, either. He managed to get him to the top of the steps but nearly fainted from the exertion. Sick and dizzy, he viewed the prospect of lugging Mr North all the way down the steps with dismay. There was nothing else for it. Summoning up one last burst of energy, he launched Mr North off the top steps with a grunting shove. Gravity did the rest. Mr North banged, bounced and barrel-rolled down the steps, fetching up at their foot in a gangling, insensible heap.

The man, on his knees, waited for his head to clear and his heart to stop thumping. Eventually, he was able to stand up and close and lock the door. He made his way back along the passageway to the bookcase, tugged the lever, and emerged, on unsteady legs, into Mr North's study.

There he found the rat. It was squatting on the mantelshelf, just above the hook for the cellar key, as if it wanted to show the man how clever it had been to scale the mantelshelf and detach the key from the hook. The man scratched its head for a while, the rat half-closing its eyes in pleasure.

'You're pretty much finished here, aren't you?' he said to it. 'Your work's done. You're back off to where you came from, wherever that is.' He forced his inflamed, lumpen lips into a smile. 'Thanks, little friend. I'm going to miss you.'

The rat gave the man's fingertip a playful, affectionate little nip, as though for old times' sake, then raced off along the mantelshelf, dangled over the end, dropped to the floor, and vanished between two bookcases.

The man hung the key back on the hook, remembering how the rat had brought it to him earlier that day. He had been surprised at first that the rat had not waited till their usual rendezvous time, but then, running his fingertips over the contours of the key in the dark, he had realised that the break from routine made sense. The rat could not have brought the key any later. Otherwise Mr North would have come home, discovered it missing, and then the game would have been up.

When he had sufficiently recovered his strength, he set about exploring the mansion. That afternoon he had ventured no further than the study, for there had been domestic staff everywhere else. Now, alone, he roamed the vastness of the building, wandering through its numerous bedrooms, its winding corridors, its majestic halls and spiralling staircases, its recreation rooms, its luxuriously appointed bathrooms, the whole gilt and splendour of the place. He gazed out at the night views: a clear moon and intermittent, silver-edged clouds, lawns patterned with slanting lozenges of window-glow, dark trees – oaks among them, no doubt – and, far off, a row of hills, black against the deep starry blue of the sky. He found a well-stocked first aid kit and constructed a splint for his fingers using bandages and tongue depressors, then fixed himself a meal in the kitchen. When he had eaten, he gathered up armfuls of dry goods and bottled water from the pantry and carried them to the cellar door. Having first established that Mr North was still unconscious, he piled up the supplies next to the mattress. Even in the dark, Mr North would find them soon enough.

He ran a deep bath, filled it with scents and oils, and soaked in it for an hour. He scrubbed himself clean and washed the dirty, tangled mass of his hair half a dozen times, using up an entire bottle of shampoo. With a pair of scissors, he stood before the bathroom mirror and hacked off his damp, straggling locks, cropping close to his scalp. He chopped off most of his beard as well, and shaved the rest with a razor. Then he presented himself before the mirror again.

The man who stared back at him was gaunt and pale and battered and haggard, but still unmistakably, undeniably, William Ian North.

He spent the most comfortable night of his life in Mr North's double-divan, beneath Mr North's eiderdown duvet, wearing Mr North's silk pyjamas. Come dawn, he was up and about. It wouldn't do to waste the day.

He dressed in a set of Mr North's casual clothes and went around the house again and also the grounds, familiarising himself with every aspect of Mr North's domestic existence. He revelled in the taste and smell of outdoor air, the glitter of dew on the grass, the twitter of bird-song. He wandered, sometimes giggling to himself.

The liberty to move unconstrained seemed a gift of incalculable value. The sky was immense and infinite. There was almost more brightness and detail than his eyes could cope with.

And inside the mansion, too, there were delights to be cherished. Television, stereos, an indoor swimming pool, a collection of fine wines. Such things were familiar to the man from his memories, but he also felt as if he was experiencing them for the first time. He luxuriated and self-indulged, and went to bed as gorged and giddy as a child after a birthday party.

Sunday was a day of rest, a day of retrenchment. The man soberly contemplated his next move. He was growing comfortable within the skin of Mr North. He was beginning to regard himself as William Ian North. Things he did not know about Mr North's existence he was able to intuit. For instance, he could not have known that Mr North was able to call on the services of an expert beautician twenty-four hours a day, seven days a week, but somehow he assumed this would be the case, and having looked up the beautician's phone number in Mr North's electronic personal organiser (which again, intuitively, he knew how to operate) he summoned her to the mansion.

She did not hide her shock at his appearance, but when he explained that he had been thrown from a horse yesterday – for he knew that Mr North had stables – she took his injuries in her stride and set about tidying him up. She manicured his nails, wondering aloud how he had managed to let them fall into such a state of disrepair in a little over a week. She showed him how to touch up his facial bruises with foundation so that they would be less noticeable. She called a friend of hers, a hairstylist, who came round and tidied up his hair. He apologised for its condition, saying he had thought he might be able to trim it himself and save himself some money. The beautician and the hairstylist – assuming, as most people do, that eccentricity is innate in the incredibly wealthy – accepted this excuse without batting an eyelid.

When they were gone, he examined himself in a mirror.

No one would be able to tell.

Eleven

It was another merely magnificent Monday in the life of William Ian North.

On the way into London, he chatted with the chauffeur, while Wagner played and the Tokyo index scrolled by all but ignored. The chauffeur was initially startled to have his opinion consulted on matters as diverse as bond options and the correct choice of sock-colour, but he soon got into the swing of things, and even dared to share with his uncharacteristically jolly employer a mildly blue joke he had been told in the pub on Saturday night. He assumed that the riding accident with which his boss accounted for his injuries had also knocked a few braincells loose. North, he was sure, would be back to his usual intense, taciturn self within a day or so.

The security guards at the NorthStar International Building saluted their boss as he walked in, and were informed that in future there would be no need for such formalities. In his office, North reclined in his desk chair and simply admired the view of the City for a while. Then, with an eye on the red line on the widescreen TV, he set about dismantling NorthStar International assest by asset.

By morning's end, he was worth about half as much as he had been when he started. Worried calls were coming in over the telelink. What was going on? Underlings were knocking at his door but none was invited to come in.

Lunch was a silent, perplexed affair. The other diners at the boardroom table did not broach the subject, but you could see it in their eyes: bewilderment bordering on fear. Had the boss gone mad? He was selling off holdings at a small fraction of their worth, incurring unthinkable quantities of Capital Gains Tax in the process. Management consortia were forming and making ridiculously low bids for ownership of his companies, and he was accepting them. Subsidiary parts of North-Star International were being entrusted solely to their administrative boards. North had, it seemed, let go of the steering wheel, and the car wasn't simply careering out of control, it was falling to bits as well.

North ate lavishly. His subordinates barely touched their food.

He rested well, and the woman who came to see him at three was bemused, and perhaps a little flattered, by the hymns to her beauty that North sang before, during and after coitus. He seemed somehow less mature and less experienced than she remembered. Like the chauffeur, she ascribed the change in personality to a knock on the head, and thought no more of it.

Markets across the world seesawed dramatically as the piecemeal disintegration of NorthStar International went on. The structure that had been built, to a large extent, on the clone-golem's pain, was coming apart, brick by brick. The process continued over the next few days. By the end of the week, there was barely a NorthStar International left. The company was still trading, but ninety per cent of its workforce had moved across into other jobs or were now running smaller, independent outfits, answerable only to themselves, responsible for their own successes and failures.

In Latin America, the Far East, Europe, the United States, everywhere, people – even people who had no direct connection with NorthStar International – were left wondering what had happened. Without knowing quite why, they sensed that, somewhere, some huge, obstructing blockage had been cleared. There was chaos, but within the chaos new shapes could be discerned like figures in mist. World-wide, there was a sense of trepidation and, at the same time, jubilation.

Twelve

North had no idea how long the door had been open. His captor must have unlocked it while he had been asleep.

He climbed the steps and tottered into the passageway. He opened the bookcase and walked, blinking, into his study. What day was it? How long had he been a prisoner? He had tried to keep track of time by rationing out the food and water that the clone-golem had left him, using the circadian rhythms of hunger as his guide, but the method did not work because he had no idea how long he had been unconscious to begin with and because the trauma of captivity destroyed his appetite. In a timeless, benighted limbo he had alternately screamed with panic, pecked at food, stood at the door pounding and begging for release, curled up on the floor whimpering, and fleetingly and sporadically slept. For how many days had he existed in this wretched state? Three, he estimated. Four at the most.

He was shocked to discover, via the television, that it was a Friday. A week. He had been down in the cellar for a whole week.

Where was the clone-golem? Where had he got to? What had he done while he had been keeping North in the cellar?

North found out soon enough by accessing his accounts from the computer in his study. And as he surveyed the ruin of his empire, he felt a solitary, humiliating kind of grief. The loss gutted him. At the same time, however, he felt a peculiar sensation of lightness. It was as though, having had so much gouged out of him financially, he actually weighed less.

The clone-golem had left him with enough to live on in reasonable comfort. The mansion was still his. The chauffeur would not have to go, although the stables and the golf course were now under public proprietorship. Things were not *so* bad.

In examining the state of his finances, North also found that monies had been diverted to an anonymous Swiss bank account. The sum was exactly the same amount as the clone-golem had left him for his own use.

At midnight, he went to the window and peered out into the darkness.

He was out there somewhere. The man who had his face, his DNA, his memories. Out there, roaming the world. Exploring. Discovering. Exulting in his freedom.

North's instinctive urge was to have him tracked down. Set the very best and most expensive private detectives he could find on the clone-golem's trail. It wouldn't take long. Whatever steps the clone-golem took to disguise his appearance, people would always note someone who bore a marked resemblance to William Ian North. He would be found and brought back to England to face North's full wrath. Money would be no object . . .

But of course, money *was* an object, now that North had comparatively little of it. And besides, for some strange reason North could not bring himself to hate the clone-golem. It seemed incomprehensible to him, after what the clone-golem had done to him, but he could find in himself no great desire to recapture the creature and begin the whole cycle of achievement and beatings all over again. Down in the cellar he had had a taste of what he had put the clone-golem through. He had suffered nowhere near as grievously as the clone-golem had suffered . . . but the experience had been bad enough. He now knew the true price at which his success had been bought.

The clone-golem had, under the circumstances, treated him with undeserved mercy. The least he could do was return the favour.

Solemnly staring out into the night, William Ian North – in what was probably the first genuinely charitable act of his life – wished the creature happiness.